THE HAUNTED POOL

THE HAUNTED POOL

(LA MARE AU DIABLE)

From the French of GEORGE SAND

BY

FRANK HUNTER POTTER

Illustrated with Fourteen Etchings by RUDAUX

ISBN: 0-915288-26-5
Library of Congress # 76-017785
This edition copyright © 1976 Shameless Hussy Press

3rd printing

Shameless Hussy Press
Box 424
San Lorenzo, California 94580

NOTICE.

WHEN I began, with "The Haunted Pool," a
series of rustic tales which I purposed col-
lecting under the title of "Tales of a Hemp-Dresser,"
I had no system, no design of revolutionizing literature. No one makes a revolution by himself; and
there are some revolutions, especially in the arts,
which humanity accomplishes without quite knowing how, because it is everybody who takes them
in hand. But this is not applicable to the romance
of rural manners: it has existed in all ages and in
all forms, sometimes pompous, sometimes affected,
sometimes simple. I have said, and must here repeat, that the dream of a country life has always
been the ideal of cities and even of courts. I have
done nothing new in following the declivity which

leads civilized man back to the charms of primitive life. I have not wished either to create a new language or to seek a new style, yet I have been told so in a goodly number of articles ; but I know better than any one else what is true about my own intentions, and I am always astonished that criticism seeks so far, when the simplest idea, the commonest circumstance, are the only inspirations to which art products owe their being. As for " The Haunted Pool " in particular, the fact which I have related in the preface, — an engraving by Holbein, which had struck me, and a real scene which I had before my eyes at the same moment, in seed-time, — this is all that prompted me to write this modest story, the scene of which has been laid amid the humble landscapes through which I passed every day. If I am asked what I wished to do, I will reply that I wished to do something very touching and simple, and that I have not succeeded to my own satisfaction. I have indeed seen and felt the beautiful in the simple, but to see and to paint are not the same thing. The best that an artist can hope is to persuade those who have eyes to look also. Do you, therefore, see simplicity, — see the sky and the fields and the trees and the peasants, above all, in that which is good and true in them. You will see them a little in my book; you will see them much better in nature.

GEORGE SAND.

Nohant, April 12, 1851.

THE HAUNTED POOL.

I.

A la sueur de ton visaige
Tu gagnerois ta pauvre vie.
Après long travail et usaige,
Voicy la *mort* qui te convie.[1]

THE quatrain, in old French, placed beneath a composition by Holbein, is profoundly sad in its quaint simplicity. The engraving represents a laborer ploughing in a field. A vast plain stretches into the distance, and upon it are seen poor cabins; the sun is setting behind a hill. It is the end of a day of hard work. The peasant is old, sturdy, clad in rags. The team of four horses which he urges before him is thin

[1] By the sweat of thy weary face
Thou shalt maintain thy wretched life.
After labor long and strife,
See! death calls thee to thy place.

and worn out; the ploughshare sinks into a rugged and stubborn soil. Only one being is brisk and active in this scene of "sweat and labor." It is a fantastic character, a skeleton armed with a whip, running in the furrow beside the frightened horses and beating them, thus serving as a plough-boy to the old laborer. It is Death, that spectre which Holbein has introduced allegorically in that succession of philosophical and religious subjects, at once mournful and grotesque, entitled "The Dance of Death."

In this collection, or rather in this vast composition in which Death, playing its role upon every page, is the connecting link and dominating thought, Holbein shows us sovereigns, pontiffs, lovers, gamblers and drunkards, nuns and courtesans, brigands, beggars and warriors, monks, Jews, and travellers,— the whole society of his time and our own; and everywhere the spectre of Death gibes, threatens, and triumphs. From but one picture is it absent. It is that in which the beggar Lazarus, lying upon a dung-heap at the rich man's gate, declares that he does not fear him, no doubt because he has nothing to lose, and his life is a premature death.

Is this stoic thought of the semi-pagan Christianity of the Renaissance very consoling, and do religious souls find in it what they need? The ambitious man and the swindler, the tyrant and the debauchee, and all those proud sinners who abuse life, and whom Death holds by the hair, will be punished, no doubt; but are the blind man and the beggar, the maniac and the poor peasant, repaid for their long misery by the mere reflection that death is not an ill for them? No! A pitiless *sadness, a frightful fatality, weighs upon the artist's work. It resembles a bitter malediction launched against the fate of humanity.*

That is indeed the painful satire, the true painting of society which Holbein had before his eyes. Crime and misfortune were all that struck him; but what shall we, the artists of another age, paint? Shall we seek in the thought of death the remuneration of present humanity? Shall we look to it as the punishment of injustice and the compensation for suffering?

No; we no longer have to do with death, but with life. We no longer believe either in annihilation in the tomb or in a salvation purchased by a forced renunciation; we wish life to be happy because we wish it to be fertile. Lazarus must leave his dung-heap, in order that the poor may no longer rejoice at the death of the rich. All must be happy, so that the happiness of a few may not be criminal and accursed of God. The laborer, as he sows his wheat, must know that he is toiling at the work of life, and not rejoice because death stalks by his side. In short, death must no longer be either the penalty for prosperity or the consolation of misery. God did not destine it to be either the punishment or the compensation for life; for he has blessed life, and the tomb ought not to be a refuge to which we are permitted to send those whom we do not wish to make happy.

Certain artists of our time, casting a serious look upon what surrounds them, devote themselves to painting wretchedness, the abjectness of poverty, Lazarus's dung-heap. This may belong to the domain of art and philosophy; but when they paint poverty so hideous and degraded, sometimes so vicious and criminal, do they attain their end, and is the effect wholesome, as they would have it? We will not venture to decide upon this point. It may be said that by showing this chasm beneath the fragile soil of opulence, they frighten the wicked rich man, as in the time of the " Danse Macabre" they showed him his yawning grave, and Death ready to enfold him in his obscene embrace. Now they show him the burglar picking the lock of his door, and the assassin spying upon his slumbers. We confess that we do not understand very clearly how they will reconcile him with humanity, which he despises, or make him pity the distresses of the beggar whom he dreads, by showing him this beggar under the form of a housebreaker or an escaped convict. That frightful Death, grinning and playing the fiddle in the pictures of Holbein and his predecessors, did not succeed, under this aspect, in converting the wicked and consoling the victims. Is not our literature proceeding in this somewhat like the artists of the Middle Ages and the Renaissance ?

Holbein's topers fill their cups with a kind of fury, in order to drive away the thought of Death, who, invisible to them, acts as their cup-bearer. The wicked rich men of our day ask for cannon and fortifications, to ward off the idea of a Jacquerie, which Art shows to them laboring insidiously in the darkness, waiting for the moment to fall upon the organization of society. The Church of the Middle Ages replied to the terrors of the mighty of the earth by the sale of indulgences. The government of to-day calms the anxiety of the rich by

making them pay for numbers of policemen and gaolers, bay-
onets and prisons.

Albert Durer, Michael Angelo, Holbein, Callot, and Goya
have made powerful satires upon the ills of their times and
their countries. Theirs are immortal works, historical pages
of incontestable value. We do not wish to deny artists the
right to probe the sores of society and to reveal them to our
eyes, but is there not something to do now other than to paint
pictures which appall and threaten? In this literature of the
mysteries of iniquity, which talent and imagination have
made the fashion, we prefer the gentle, sweet characters to
the dramatic villains. The former can undertake and accom-
plish conversions, the latter terrify; and fear does not cure
egotism, it increases it.

We believe that the mission of Art is a mission of sentiment and love, that the romance of to-day should replace the
parable and the apologue of primitive times, and that the
artist has a wider and more poetic task than that of propos-
ing a few measures of prudence and conciliation to diminish
the dread inspired by his pictures. His end ought to be to
cause the objects of his solicitude to be loved, and I should not
find fault with him for beautifying them a little, if need
were. Art is not a study of positive reality, it is the seeking for ideal truth; and the " Vicar of Wakefield" was a
more useful and more wholesome book than the " Paysan
Perverti" or the " Liaisons Dangereuses."

Reader, forgive me for these reflections, and be good
enough to accept them as a preface. There will be none in
the little tale which I am going to tell you, and it will be so

short and so simple that I needed to excuse myself in advance
by telling you what I think of terrible stories.

It is in connection with a laborer that I have allowed
myself to be drawn into this digression. It is the story of a
laborer which I intended to tell you, and which I will tell
in a moment.

II.

PLOUGHING.

I HAD been looking for a long while and with profound
melancholy at Holbein's ploughman, and I was walking
in the country, pondering over life in the fields and the
destiny of the husbandman. It is sad, no doubt, to exhaust
one's strength and one's days in cleaving the bosom of this
jealous earth, which compels us to wring from it the treasures of its fertility, when a bit of the blackest and coarsest
bread is, at the end of the day's work, the sole recompense
and the sole profit attaching to so arduous a toil. This
wealth which covers the ground, these harvests and fruits,
these splendid beasts fattening in the long grass, are the
property of a few, and the instruments of the fatigue and

slavery of the greater number. The man of leisure does not generally love for their own sake either fields or meadows, the sight of Nature or the superb animals which are to be converted into gold pieces for his use. He comes to seek a little air and health in a visit to the country, and then returns to spend in great cities the fruit of his vassals' labor.

On the other hand, the toiler is too dejected, too wretched, and too fearful of the future to enjoy the beauty of the country and the charms of rustic life. For him, also, the golden fields, the lovely meadows, the handsome cattle represent bags of gold of which he will have but a small part, insufficient for his needs; nevertheless, he must fill these accursed sacks every year in order to satisfy the master and to buy the right to live frugally and wretchedly upon his land.

Yet Nature is eternally young, beautiful, and generous. She sheds poetry and beauty upon all beings, upon all plants which are allowed to develop fully in the country. She possesses the secret of happiness, and no one has been able to steal it from her. The happiest of men would be he who, working intelligently and laboring with his hands, drawing comfort and liberty from the exercise of his intelligent strength, should have time to live through his heart and his brain, to comprehend his own work and that of God. The artist has enjoyments of this kind in the contemplation and reproduction of the beauties of Nature; but when he sees the wretchedness of the men who people this earthly paradise, the artist with an upright and humane soul is troubled in the midst of his enjoyment. Happiness would be wherever the mind, the heart, and the arm should work together beneath the eye of Providence, so that a holy harmony should exist between the munificence of God and the rapture of the human soul. Then, instead of a pitiful and frightful Death stalking whip in hand along the furrow, the allegorical painter might set by the laborer's side a radiant angel, sowing the blessed wheat broadcast over the smoking soil.

And the dream of a sweet, free, poetic, laborious, and simple life for the tiller of the soil is not so difficult to conceive that it need be dismissed as a chimera. Virgil's sad but sweet words, " Oh, happy the man of the fields, if he but knew his happiness ! " are a regret; but like all regrets, they are also a prediction. A day will come when the husbandman will be able to be an artist also, — if not to express (which will then matter little enough), at least to feel the beautiful. Does any one suppose that this mysterious intuition of poetry is not already in him in the condition of an instinct and a vague revery? Among those who are already protected by a little wealth, and in whom excessive wretchedness does not stifle all moral and intellectual developments, pure, conscious, and appreciated happiness exists in an elementary state. Besides, if from the abodes of wretchedness and weariness poets' voices have already risen, why should it be said that manual labor precludes the functions of the soul? No doubt this preclusion is the general result of excessive toil and abject poverty; but let it not be said that when man shall work moderately and usefully there shall be none but bad workmen and bad poets. He who draws noble delights from the sentiment of poetry is a true poet, though he has never written a line in all his life.

My thoughts had taken this course, and I did not perceive that this confidence in man's capacity for education was strengthened in me by exterior influences. I was walking along the edge of a field which the peasants were preparing for the forthcoming sowing. The enclosure was as large as that in Holbein's picture. The landscape also was broad; and it framed, with lines of verdure somewhat reddened by approaching autumn, this vast field of a lusty brown, upon which recent rains had left in a few furrows lines of water which the sun made to glisten like slender threads of silver. The day was clear and warm, and the soil, newly opened by the stroke of the plough, exhaled a slight vapor. At the top of the field an old man, whose broad back and severe face recalled Holbein's ploughman, but whose garments did not proclaim poverty, was gravely driving his plough of antique shape, drawn by two calm oxen with hides of a pale yellow, — true patriarchs of the meadow, tall, somewhat thin, with long, drooping horns, — those old work-cattle which long habit has made " brothers," as they are called by our peasants, and which, when one loses the other, refuse to work with a new companion, and allow themselves to die of sorrow. People who do not know the country say that the friendship of an ox for his yoke-fellow is a fable. Let them come and see in some dark corner of a stable a poor, thin, worn-out animal, beating its lean flanks with its restless tail, snorting with fright and contempt at the food which is offered it, with its eyes always turned toward the door, pawing the empty place at its side, sniffing at the yokes and chains which its companion has worn, and ceaselessly calling it with lamentable lowings. The oxherd will say: " There are a pair of oxen lost; his brother is dead, and this one will never work again. We ought to fatten him to kill; but he will not eat, and soon he will be dead of hunger."

The old laborer was working slowly, silently, without unnecessary effort. His docile team hurried no more than he did; but thanks to the continuity of a labor without distraction, and an expenditure of tried and sustained strength, his furrow was ploughed as soon as that of his son, who was driving, a little way off, four less vigorous oxen in a more stony and stubborn vein of earth.

But what next attracted my attention was a really fine spectacle, — a subject worthy of a painter. At the opposite end of the arable plain a good-looking young man was driving a magnificent team, — four pairs of young animals with mingled black and tawny hides which gave out glints as of fire, with those short and curly heads which still show the wild bull, and those great wild eyes, those sudden movements, that nervous and abrupt manner of working, still resenting the yoke and the goad, and only obeying with quiverings of anger a recently imposed authority. They were what are called " newly yoked " oxen.

The man who drove them had to break up a corner which had formerly been given up to pasture and which was filled with old roots, — an arduous task for which his energy, his youth, and his eight almost wild cattle were hardly sufficient.

A child between six and seven years old, handsome as an angel, and with his shoulders covered above his blouse with a lamb-skin which caused him to resemble the little Saint John Baptist of the painters of the Renaissance, was walking in the furrow beside the plough, and pricking the flanks of the oxen with a long, light goad with a dull point. The proud animals quivered beneath the child's little hand, and made the yokes and the straps fastened to their brows creak, shaking the pole violently. When a root stopped the ploughshare, the laborer would cry out with a powerful voice, calling each animal by his name, but rather to quiet than to excite them; for the oxen, irritated by this sudden resistance, would spring forward, tearing up the ground with their cloven hoofs, and would have thrown themselves to one side, carrying the plough across the field, if the young man had not restrained the first four with voice and goad, while the child directed the other four. The poor little fellow also shouted in a voice which he wished to make terrible, and which remained as sweet as his angelic face. It was all beautiful from its strength or its grace, — the landscape, the man, the child, the oxen under the yoke; and in spite of this mighty strife in which the earth was vanquished, there was a feeling of sweetness and profound calm which

brooded over everything. When the obstacle was surmounted and the train resumed its regular and solemn
progress, the laborer, whose feigned violence was only
an exercise of strength and an expenditure of activity,
quickly resumed the serenity of a simple soul, and cast
a look of fatherly contentment upon his child, who turned
about to smile at him. Then the manly voice of this
young father would raise the solemn and melancholy
refrain which the ancient tradition of the district transmits, not to all laborers indiscriminately, but to the most
consummate in the art of exciting and sustaining the
spirit of working cattle. This song — the origin of which
was perhaps considered sacred, and to which mysterious
influences must formerly have been attributed — is still
reputed to possess the virtue of supporting the courage
of these animals, of quieting their irritation, and of charming the weariness of their long tasks. It is not enough
to know how to drive them well, tracing the furrow perfectly straight and lightening their labor by raising the
iron share or by sinking it deeper into the ground; no
one is a perfect husbandman who does not know how to
sing to his oxen, and that is a science by itself which
demands a special taste and ability.

This song is, indeed, only a kind of recitative broken
off and resumed at will. Its irregular form and its in-
tonations, which are false according to the rules of the
musical art, make it indescribable. But it is none the
less a beautiful song, and so appropriate to the nature of
the work which it accompanies, to the pace of the oxen,

to the calmness of the rustic scene, to the simplicity of
the men who sing it, that no genius unfamiliar with the
labor of the ground could have invented it, and no
singer other than a skilful husbandman of that district
could repeat it. At the periods of the year when there
is no other work or movement in the country than that
of the ploughing, this song, so sweet and so powerful,
rises like a voice of the breeze, to which its peculiar
tonality gives it a certain resemblance. The final note
of each phrase, held and shaken with an incredible length
and power of breath, rises a quarter of a tone, sharping
systematically. It is wild, but the charm of it is unspeak-
able; and when one is accustomed to hear it, one cannot
imagine how any other song could arise at these hours
and in these spots without disturbing their harmony.

It happened, therefore, that I had before my eyes a
picture which contrasted with that of Holbein, although
it was a similar scene. Instead of a sad old man there
was a young and active one; instead of a train of thin
and weary horses, four yoke of vigorous and spirited
oxen; instead of Death, a beautiful child; instead of an
image of despair and an idea of destruction, a spectacle
of energy and a thought of happiness.

It was then that the quatrain

" A la sueur de ton visaige," etc.

and the " O fortunatos . . . agricolas " of Virgil came to my
mind together, and that as I saw this handsome couple
— the man and the child — performing under such poetic
conditions and with so much grace united to their

strength a work full of grandeur and solemnity, I felt a profound pity mingled with involuntary respect. Happy the laborer! Yes; and so, no doubt, should I be in his place if my arm suddenly grown strong, and my voice become powerful, could thus fertilize and sing Nature without having my eyes cease to see and my brain to understand the harmony of colors and sounds, the delicacy of shades and the grace of outlines, — in a word, the mysterious beauty of things; and, above all, without having my heart cease to be in accordance with the divine sentiment which presided over the immortal and divine creation.

But, alas! this man has never comprehended the mystery of the beautiful, this child never will comprehend it! God preserve me from believing that they are not superior to the animals of which they are masters, and that they have not at certain moments a sort of ecstatic revelation which charms their fatigue and lulls their cares to sleep. I see upon their noble brows the seal of the Lord, for they were born kings of the earth far more truly than those who possess it only from having bought it. And the proof that they feel this is that they cannot be expatriated with impunity; that they love this earth, watered with their tears; that the true peasant dies of homesickness in the uniform of the soldier far from the fields which saw his birth. But this man lacks a part of the enjoyments which I possess, — immaterial enjoyments which are surely due to him, the workman in the great temple which the sky alone is vast enough to cover.

Those who condemned him to servitude from his mother's womb, being unable to rob him of revery, have deprived him of reflection.

Well, such as he is, incomplete and condemned to an eternal childhood, he is yet more beautiful than the man in whom knowledge has stifled sentiment. Do not raise yourselves above him, you who believe yourselves invested with the legitimate and inalienable right to command him; for this frightful error in which you are proves that your mind has killed your heart, and that you are the most incomplete and blindest of men! I prefer the simplicity of his soul to the false lights of yours; and if I had to relate his life, I should have more pleasure in bringing out its tender and touching side than you have merit in painting the abjectness into which the severity and contempt of your social precepts can cast him.

I knew this young man and this handsome child. I knew their story, for they had a story; every one has his own, and every one could arouse interest in the romance of his life if he but comprehended it. Although a peasant and a simple farm-laborer, Germain had understood his duties and his affections. He had related them to me simply and clearly, and I had listened to him with interest. When I had watched him ploughing for some time, I asked myself why his story should not be written, although it was a story as simple and straightforward and as little embellished as the furrow which he was marking with his plough.

Next year this furrow will be filled up and covered by

a new furrow. Thus are made and disappear the marks of most men in the field of humanity. A little earth effaces them, and the furrows which we have made follow one another like tombs in a cemetery. Is not the furrow of the husbandman of as great value as that of the idle man, who nevertheless has a name, — a name which will remain if because of some peculiarity or absurdity he makes a little noise in the world?

Well, let us, if possible, save from the annihilation of forgetfulness the furrow of Germain, the skilful husbandman. He will know nothing of it, and care little, and I shall have had some pleasure in attempting it.

III.

FATHER MAURICE

"GERMAIN," his father-in-law one day said to him, "you really must make up your mind to take another wife. It is nearly two years since you lost my daughter, and your eldest boy is seven years old. You are close to thirty, my lad, and you know that after that age a man is considered in our neighborhood too old to marry again. You have three fine children, and thus far they have not been a trouble to us. My wife and my daughter-in-law have cared for them as well as they could, and have loved them as they ought. Little Pierre is almost grown up; he already drives oxen nicely enough;

he is sufficiently well behaved to take care of the cattle in the pasture, and strong enough to lead the horses to water. Therefore it is not he who troubles us, but the two others, — whom we love, however, God knows! The poor little things have given us a good deal of anxiety this year. My daughter-in-law will shortly be confined, and she already has a very little child on her hands. When the one for which we are waiting comes, she will no longer be able to attend to your little Solange, and especially to your Sylvain, who is not yet four, and who is hardly still for a moment, day or night. His blood is fiery, like yours; he will make a good workman, but he is a terrible child, and my old wife cannot move fast enough to catch him when he runs away toward the ditch or throws himself under the feet of the cattle. And then, with this other which my daughter-in-law is about to bring into the world, the care of her next older child will fall upon my wife for at least a year. Consequently your children overburden us and make us anxious. We do not like to see children ill cared for, and when we think of the accidents which may happen to them for lack of watching, our minds are never at ease. You must therefore have another wife and I another daughter-in-law. Think about it, my lad. I have already warned you several times; time flies, and the years will not wait for you. You owe it to your children and to us, who wish to have everything go well in the house, to marry as soon as possible."

"Well, father," replied the son-in-law, " if you wish it

absolutely, I must do as you will. But I do not care to conceal from you that it will pain me greatly, and that I had almost as lief drown myself. One knows what one has lost, but not what one may find. I had a good wife, handsome, sweet, brave, — good to her father and mother, her husband and children, — a good worker in the field as in the house, skilful, — good in every way, in short; and when you gave her to me, when I married her, it was not part of the bargain that I should forget her if I had the misfortune to lose her."

" What you say shows a good heart, Germain," returned Father Maurice. " I know that you loved my daughter, that you made her happy, and that if you could have satisfied Death by taking her place, Catherine would be alive now, and you in the cemetery. She richly deserved to be so loved by you; and if you are not consoled for her loss, neither are we. But I do not tell you to forget her. The good Lord wished her to leave us; and not a day passes without our letting her know, by our prayers and thoughts, our words and deeds, that we respect her memory and are grieved at her departure. But if she could speak to you from the other world and give you to know her will, she would command you to seek a mother for her little orphans. We must try, therefore, to find a woman who is worthy to replace her. It will not be very easy, but it will not be impossible; and when we shall have found her for you, you will love her as you loved my daughter, because you are an honest man, and you will be grateful to her for doing us a service and for loving your children."

"Very good, Father Maurice," said Germain; "I will do your will, as I have always done it."

"I must do you the justice to say, my son, that you have always listened to the friendly advice and the good reasons of the head of your family. Let us consult, therefore, about the choice of your new wife. In the first place, I do not think that you ought to take a very young woman. That is not what you need. Youth is flighty; and as it is a burden to bring up three children, especially when they spring from another marriage, you need a good soul, very sensible, very gentle, and very fond of work. If your wife is not of about your own age, she will not be reasonable enough to accept such a duty. She will think you too old, and your children too young. She will think herself to be pitied, and your children will suffer."

"That is precisely what troubles me," said Germain. "Suppose the poor little things were to be maltreated, hated, beaten?"

"God forbid!" replied the old man. "But ill-natured women are rarer in our neighborhood than good ones, and we should have to be mad not to lay hands on one who will suit you."

"It is true, father; there are good women in our village. There are Louise, Sylvaine, Claudie, Marguerite, — in short, whichever you like."

"Gently, gently, my lad; all these girls are too young, or too poor — or too pretty; for we must think of that also, my son. A pretty woman is not always so steady as another."

"Then you wish me to marry an ugly one?" said Germain, a little uneasy.

"No, not ugly; for this woman will bear you other children, and there is nothing so sad as to have ugly, weak, and unhealthy children. But a woman who is still fresh, with good health, and neither handsome nor ugly, would be about what you need."

"I see," said Germain, smiling somewhat sadly, "that for her to suit you, she will have to be made to order; especially as you do not want her to be poor, and rich ones are not easy to get, above all for a widower."

"And suppose she were a widow herself, Germain, — a widow without children and with a good property?"

"I do now know of any just now in our parish."

"Nor I either, but they are to be found elsewhere."

"You have some one in view, father? Then say so at once."

IV.

GERMAIN.

"YES, I have some one in view," replied Father Maurice. "She is a Léonard, the widow of a Guérin, and lives at Fourche."

"I do not know either the woman or the place," replied Germain, resigned, but more and more sad.

"She is named Catherine, like her whom you have lost."

"Catherine? Yes, it will give me pleasure to have to speak that name, — Catherine! And yet, if I cannot love her so much as the other, it will give me still greater pain, for it will remind me of her more often."

"I tell you that you will love her; she is a good creature, a woman with a warm heart. I have not seen her for a long time; she was not an ugly girl then, but she is no longer young, — she is two-and-thirty. She comes of a good family, all honest folk, and she has some eight or ten thousand francs' worth of land, which she would willingly sell, to buy other property in the neighborhood in which she might settle; for she also is thinking of marrying again, and I know that if your character suited her, she would not find fault with your position."

"Then you have already arranged it all?"

"Yes, except for the opinion of you two; and that is what you must ask one another, by becoming acquainted. The father of this woman is a distant relative of mine, and has been a close friend. You surely know him, — Father Léonard?"

"Yes, I have seen him talking to you at the fairs, and at the last one you breakfasted together. So that is what he talked to you about so long?"

"Precisely; he was watching you sell your cattle, and he thought that you managed it well, that you were a good-looking fellow, and that you appeared active and intelligent. And when I told him what you are, and how well you have behaved toward us during the eight years that we have lived and worked together, without ever having a word of complaint or anger, he took it into his head to have you marry his daughter. And it suits me also, I confess, considering her good reputation, the honesty of her family, and the prosperous condition in which I know them to be."

"I see, Father Maurice, that you care for the prosperous condition."

"Certainly I do. Do not you care for it also?"

"I care for it if you wish, to please you; but you know that, for my part, I am never concerned about what part of our profits does or does not come to me. I do not understand accounts, and have no head for them. I understand land; I am a judge of cattle, horses, and carts; I know about sowing, threshing, and forage. As for the sheep, the vineyard, the garden, the small profits and fine culture, you know that your son attends to that, and I do not meddle much with it. As for money, my memory is short, and I would rather give up everything than dispute about mine and thine. I should be afraid of making a mistake and claiming what was not my due; and if business matters were not clear and simple, I should never be able to find my way in them."

"So much the worse, my son; and that is why I should like you to have a wife with a good head to replace me when I am gone. You have never been willing to understand our accounts, and this might bring about disagreements with my son when you no longer have me to keep you in harmony and to tell you how much comes to each of you."

"I hope you may live a long while, Father Maurice. But do not be anxious about what may happen after your time; I shall never quarrel with your son. I trust to Jacques as to yourself, and as I have no property of my own, and all that could come to me comes from your daughter and belongs to our children, I can be easy, and you also. Jacques would not rob his sister's children for his own, since he loves them all almost equally."

" You are right in that, Germain. Jacques is a good son, a good brother, and a man who loves the truth. But Jacques may die before you, and before your children are grown up; and we must always think, in a family, of not leaving minors without a head to counsel them wisely and to settle their differences. Otherwise the lawyers meddle, set them to quarrelling, and make them eat up everything in lawsuits. Consequently we must not think of bringing among us another person, man or woman, without remembering that some day this person may have to direct the conduct and manage the affairs of twenty or thirty children and grandchildren, sons-in-law and daughters-in-law. One never knows how much a family may grow; and when a hive is too full, and it is necessary to form a new swarm, each one thinks of carrying away his own honey. When I took you for a son-in-law, although my daughter was rich and you were poor, I did not reproach her for having chosen you. I saw that you were a good worker, and I knew that the best wealth for country people like us was such a pair of arms and such a heart as yours. When a man brings that into a family he brings enough. But with a woman it is different; her work in the household serves to keep, not to acquire. Besides, now that you are a father and are seeking a wife, you must remember that your future children, having no claim upon the inheritance of those of the former marriage, would find themselves penniless if you were to die, unless your wife had some property of her own. And then the children with which you will increase our colony will cost something to feed. If that were to fall upon us alone we should feed them, certainly, and without complaining; but the comfort of every one would be diminished, and your first children would have their share in these privations. When families grow immoderately without a proportionate increase of property, poverty follows, no matter how brave one may be. That is what I had to say, Germain; weigh it, and try to make the Widow Guérin like you, for her good behavior and her money will bring to this place aid for the present and tranquillity for the future."

"Very good, father. I will try to please her and to have her please me."

"For that you must go to see her."

"Where she lives? At Fourche? It is a long way from here, is it not? and we have little time for gadding at this season."

"When it is a question of a love-match, one must expect to lose time; but when it is a marriage of reason between two people who have no fancies and know what they want, matters are quickly settled. To-morrow will be Saturday; you will do a short day's ploughing, and start about two in the afternoon. You will reach Fourche in the evening. The moon is full just now, the roads are good, and it is not more than three of our leagues. It is near Le Magnier. Besides, you will take the mare."

"I would a little rather go on foot in this cool weather."

"Yes; but the mare is handsome, and a suitor who arrives so well mounted has a better appearance. You must wear your new clothes, and you can take a nice present of game to Father Léonard. You will come from me, you will talk to him and spend Sunday with his daughter, and you can come back with a yes or a no on Monday morning."

"All right," replied Germain, quietly; and yet he was not altogether at ease.

Germain had always lived chastely, after the manner of industrious peasants. Married at twenty, he had never loved any one but his wife; and since his widowhood, although he was of a gay and impetuous character, he had never jested or sported with any other. He had faithfully kept a real regret in his heart, and it was not without fear and sadness that he yielded to his father-in-law; but the old man had ever governed the family wisely, and Germain, who had devoted himself wholly to the common work, and consequently to him who personified it, the head of the family, — Germain did not understand that he might have acted contrary to his good reason and the common interest.

Nevertheless he was sad. There were few days when he did not weep for his wife in secret; and although loneliness began to weigh heavily upon him, he was more afraid of forming a new union than of escaping from his unhappiness. He said to himself, in a vague way, that love might have consoled him by taking him by surprise; for that is the only way in which love does console. One cannot find it when one seeks it; it comes to us when we do not expect it. This cold project of marriage which Father Maurice revealed to him, this unknown betrothed, perhaps even all the good which was told him concerning her sense and virtue set him to thinking. And he went away musing as men muse who have not ideas enough for them to strive among themselves; that is to say, not formulating for himself fine reasons for selfishness and resistance, yet suffering from a dull grief, and not struggling against an ill which must needs be borne.

Meanwhile Father Maurice had returned to the farm, while Germain, between sundown and dark, spent the last hour of the day in closing the gaps which the sheep had made in the fence of an enclosure near the farm buildings. He set up the stalks of thorn-tree, and supported them with clods of earth, while the thrushes warbled in the neighboring thicket and seemed to call to him to make haste, for they were curious to come and examine his work as soon as he should go.

V.

FATHER MAURICE found at his house an old neighbor who had come to chat with his wife and at the same time to get a few live coals with which to kindle her fire. Mother Guillette dwelt in a poor cottage a couple of gun-shots' distance from the farm. But she was an orderly and hard-working woman. Her little house was clean and well kept, and her carefully patched garments proclaimed a respect for herself amid her poverty.

"You have come for your evening fire, Mother Guillette?" said the old man. "Would you like anything else?"

"No, Father Maurice," she replied, "not for the moment. I am not fond of begging, as you know, and I do not abuse the kindness of my friends."

"That is true, and therefore your friends are always ready to do you a service."

"I was just talking to your wife, and asking her whether Germain had at last decided to marry again."

"You are not a gossip," replied Father Maurice; "one can talk before you without fear of having things repeated. Consequently, I will tell my wife and you that Germain has quite decided; to-morrow he is going to the farm at Fourche."

"Good!" cried Mother Maurice. "Poor fellow! Heaven send that he find a wife as good and as honest as himself."

"Ah! he is going to Fourche?" remarked Guillette. "How lucky that is! It will just suit me; and since you asked me a moment ago if I wanted anything, I will tell you, Father Maurice, how you can oblige me."

"Tell us, tell us; we shall be glad to oblige you."

"I should like to have Germain take my daughter with him."

"Where? To Fourche?"

"No, not to Fourche, but to Les Ormeaux, where she is to remain for the rest of the year."

"What!" said Mother Maurice, "you are going to part from your daughter?"

"She must take a situation and earn something. It pains me deeply, and her too, poor soul! We could not make up our minds to part at St. John's Day; but now St. Martin's Day is coming, and she can get a good place as shepherdess at the farms at Les Ormeaux. The farmer passed here the other day on his way back from the fair. He saw

my little Marie watching her three sheep on the common. 'You have not much to do, my little girl,' said he, 'and three sheep for a shepherdess are hardly enough. Would you like to keep a hundred? I will take you with me. Our shepherdess has fallen ill, and is going home to her people; and if you will be at our place within a week you shall have fifty francs for the rest of the year, until St. John's Day.' The child refused, but she could not help thinking of it and telling me about it when upon her return in the evening she saw me sad and troubled about getting through the winter, which is going to be long and hard, since cranes and wild geese have been seen this year migrating a good month earlier than usual. We both cried, but finally we plucked up courage. We said to ourselves that we could not remain together, since there is hardly enough to support one person upon our patch of land; and since Marie is nearly grown up (she is almost sixteen), she will have to do as others do, — earn her living and help her poor mother."

"Mother Guillette," said the old farmer, "if fifty francs were all that is needed to relieve you of your troubles and spare you the necessity of sending your daughter away, I would find them for you, although fifty francs is not a trifle for people like us. But one must consider reason as much as friendship in everything. Though you might be saved from suffering this winter, you would not be spared from it in the future; and the longer your daughter delays making up her mind, the harder it will be for her and for you to part. Little Marie is growing tall and strong, and she has not enough to do at home. She might become lazy — "

"Oh, I am not afraid of that!" said Guillette. "Marie is as hard-working as a rich girl at the head of a large household could be. She never remains for an instant with folded arms; and when we have no work to do she rubs and cleans our poor furniture until she makes it as shining as a mirror. The child is worth her weight in gold, and I should have much preferred to have her come to you as shepherdess rather than go away so far among people whom I do not know. You would have taken her at St. John's Day if we could have made up our minds; but now you have hired all your hands, and we cannot think of it until St. John's Day next year."

"Oh, I consent to that with all my heart, Guillette! I shall be glad to do it. But meanwhile she will do well to learn some kind of work, and become accustomed to serve others."

"Yes, no doubt; the die is cast. The farmer at Les Ormeaux sent to ask about her this morning. We said yes, and she must go. But the poor child does not know the road, and I should not like to send her so far alone. As your son-in-law is going to Fourche to-morrow, he might take her. It appears that it is in the neighborhood of the farm to which she is going, from what I have been told; for I have never been there."

"It is quite near it, and my son-in-law will take her. That of course; he can even take her behind upon his mare, which will save her shoes. Here he is now, coming

in to supper. I say, Germain, Mother Guillette's little
Marie is going to Les Ormeaux as shepherdess. You will
take her on your horse, will you not?"

" Certainly," said Germain, who was thoughtful, but always ready to do a service to his neighbor.

In our society such a thing would not enter a mother's
mind as to intrust a girl of sixteen to a man of eight-and-
twenty; for Germain was really only twenty-eight years
old, and although, according to the ideas of his province,
he passed for old from the point of view of marriage, he
was still the handsomest man in the neighborhood. Work
had not wrinkled and withered him as it does most peasants who have worked for ten years, and the prejudice
against age must have been very strong in the mind of
a young girl to prevent her seeing that Germain had a
fresh complexion, bright eyes, blue as a May sky, a red
mouth, superb teeth, and a body elegant and supple as
that of a young horse which has never yet left the
pasture.

But chastity is a tradition in certain country districts
far removed from the corrupted life of great cities; and
among all the families of Belair that of Maurice was considered most honest and truth-serving. Germain was going to seek a wife. Marie was a child, too young and too
poor for him to think of in this light; and without being
heartless and a bad man, it was impossible for him to
have a guilty thought regarding her. Father Maurice
was therefore in no wise anxious when he saw him take
up this pretty girl behind him. Mother Guillette would

have thought she was insulting him if she had charged him to respect her like his sister. Marie mounted the mare weeping, after having embraced her mother and her young friends twenty times. Germain, who was sad for his own part, pitied her grief all the more, and went off with a serious air; while the people of the neighborhood waved a farewell to poor Marie without a thought of evil.

VI.

LITTLE PIERRE.

THE gray was young, handsome, and strong. She carried her double load without an effort, laying back her ears and champing her bit like the proud and spirited mare that she was. As she passed along the pasture she saw her mother, — who was called the old gray, as she was the young gray, — and she whinnied a good-by. The old gray came up to the hedge, clicking her shoes, and tried to gallop along the edge of the pasture to accompany her daughter; then, seeing her set off at a sharp trot, she neighed in turn, and remained thoughtful and uneasy, with her head in the air and her mouth full of grass which she never thought of eating.

"That poor creature always knows her offspring," said Germain, to divert little Marie from her sorrow. "It reminds me that I did not kiss my little Pierre before I left. The naughty child was not there! Last night he wished to make me promise to take him with me, and he cried in bed for an hour. This morning again he tried everything to persuade me. Oh, how clever and winning he is! But when he saw that it was of no use, the young gentleman got angry; he set out over the fields, and I have not seen him since."

"I saw him," said little Marie, making an effort to repress her tears. "He was running with Soulas's children in the direction of the clearing, and I suspected that he had been away from the house for a long time, for he was hungry and was eating sloes and blackberries. I gave him the bread I had for breakfast, and he said to me, 'Thank you, my little Marie; when you come to our house I will give you some cake.' He is a very lovely child, Germain."

"Yes, indeed, he is lovely," replied Germain, "and I do not know what I would not do for him. If his grandmother had not been wiser than I, I could not have helped taking him with me, when I saw him crying so hard that his poor little heart was almost broken."

"Well, why should you not have taken him with you, Germain? He is so good when one does as he wishes!"

"It seems that he would have been out of place where I am going. At least, that was Father Maurice's opinion. I, however, thought, on the contrary, that it would be well to see how he was received, and that so sweet a child could not but be kindly welcomed. But they said at home that one ought not to begin by showing the burdens of the household. I do not know why I am telling you about this, little Marie; you cannot understand it."

"Yes, Germain; I know that you are going away to get married. My mother told me so, and warned me to say nothing about it to any one, either at your house or where I am going. And you may be easy; I will not speak a word about it."

"You will do well, for it is not settled; perhaps I may not suit the woman in question."

"We must hope that you will, Germain. Why should you not suit her?"

"Who knows? I have three children, and that is a heavy burden for a woman who is not their mother."

"That is true; but your children are not like other children."

"Do you think so?"

"They are pretty as little angels, and so well brought up that one could not find nicer ones."

"Sylvain is not very easy to manage."

"He is so little! He cannot help being mischievous, but he is so clever."

"It is true that he is clever, and so brave! He is not afraid of cows or bulls; and if he were allowed he would already be clambering upon the horses with his elder brother."

" In your place I should have brought along the oldest. It would certainly have made you loved at once for having such a lovely child."

" Yes, if the woman likes children; but suppose she does not like them."

" Are there any women who do not like children? "

" Not many, I think; but still there are some, and that is what troubles me."

" Then you do not know this woman at all? "

" No more than you do; and I am afraid that I may not know her any better after having seen her. I am not distrustful. When people speak good words to me, I believe them; but I have more than once had cause to repent of it, for words are not actions."

" They say that she is a very good woman."

" Who says that? Father Maurice? "

" Yes, your father-in-law."

" That is all very well; but he does not know her either."

" Well, you will see her in a little while, you will examine her closely, and we must hope that you will not be mistaken, Germain."

" Look here, Marie, I should like it very much if you would go to the house for a while before going to Les Ormeaux. You are acute. You have always shown cleverness, and you notice everything. If you see anything which makes you doubtful, you can tell me about it quietly."

" Oh, no, Germain, I will not do that! I should be too much afraid of making a mistake. And besides, if a

word lightly spoken were to disgust you with this marriage, your people would be angry with me, and I have enough troubles already without bringing down any more upon my poor dear mother."

As they were talking thus, the gray pricked up her ears and shied, then retraced her steps and came toward the hedge, where something which she was beginning to recognize had at first frightened her. Germain cast a glance at the hedge and saw in the ditch, beneath the thick and still green branches of a scrub-oak, something which he took for a lamb.

"It is a strayed or dead animal," said he, "for it does not move."

"It is not an animal," cried little Marie; "it is a child, asleep. It is your Pierre."

"Upon my word!" said Germain, dismounting; "just see that little rascal asleep there, so far from the house, and in a ditch where a snake might find him!"

He took up the child, who smiled at him as he opened his eyes, and threw his arms about his neck, saying, "My little father, you will take me with you!"

"Ah, yes; always the same story! What were you doing there, naughty Pierre?"

"I was waiting for my little father to pass," said the child. "I looked along the road, and I looked so long that I went to sleep."

"And if I had passed without seeing you, you would have stayed out of doors all night, and the wolf would have eaten you."

"Oh, I knew that you would see me!" replied Pierre, confidently.

"Well, now, Pierre, kiss me, say good-by to me, and go back quickly to the house, if you do not wish them to have supper without you."

"You will not take me with you?" cried the child, beginning to rub his eyes, to show that he intended to cry.

"You know that grandfather and grandmother do not wish it," said Germain, intrenching himself behind the authority of the old people, like a man who does not count greatly upon his own.

But the child would not listen to anything. He began to cry in earnest, saying that since his father took Marie, he might very well take him too. They told him that they had to pass through thick woods where there were many evil beasts which ate little children, that the gray would not carry three people, that she had said so when they started, and that where they were going there would be neither bed nor supper for youngsters. All these excellent reasons did not persuade Pierre; he threw himself down upon the grass and rolled about, crying that his father no longer loved him, and that if he did not take him he would never go back to the house day nor night.

Germain had a father's heart, as tender and as weak as a woman's. The death of his wife, the care which he had been compelled to take alone of his children, as well as the thought that these poor motherless little ones needed a great deal of love, had contributed to make

him thus; and so sharp a struggle went on within him —
all the more because he blushed at his weakness and
strove to hide his discomfort from Marie — that the perspiration came to his brow and his eyes grew red, almost
ready to cry also. At last he tried to become angry; but
when he turned toward little Marie, as if to call upon her
to witness his firmness of mind, he saw that that good
girl's face was bathed in tears, and all his courage leaving him, it was impossible for him to restrain his own,
although he still scolded and threatened.

"Really, your heart is too hard," said Marie to him
at last, "and I, for my part, could never resist like that
a child who is so unhappy. Come, Germain, take him
along! Your mare is accustomed to carry two people
and a child, since your brother-in-law and his wife, who
is a great deal heavier than I, go to market on Saturdays
with their boy upon the back of this good beast. You
can mount him before you; and besides, I would rather
go on foot alone than make this child unhappy."

"Never mind that," replied Germain, who was dying
to allow himself to be convinced. "The gray is strong,
and could carry two more if there were room enough
upon her spine. But what shall we do with this child
upon the way? He will be cold and hungry, and who
will take care of him this evening and to-morrow, — put
him to bed, wash him and dress him? I dare not give
this trouble to a woman whom I do not know, and who
will think, no doubt, that I am very free with her at
the beginning."

"Believe me, Germain, you will know her at once by the pleasure or annoyance which she shows; and besides, if she will not take care of your little Pierre, I will look after him. I will go to the house to dress him, and I will take him to the fields to-morrow. I will amuse him all day, and I will see that he does not want for anything."

"And he will weary you, my poor child! He will trouble you. A whole day is a long while!"

"It will give me pleasure, on the contrary; he will keep me company and make me less sad the first day that I have to spend in a new place. I shall fancy that I am still at home."

The child, seeing that little Marie was taking his part, had seized her skirt and was clinging to it so hard that it would have been necessary to hurt him to tear him away. When he saw that his father was yielding, he took Marie's hand in his two little sunburned hands and kissed her, leaping for joy and drawing her toward the mare, with that ardent impatience which children display in their desires.

"Come, come," said the young girl, lifting him in her arms, "let us try to quiet this poor heart, which is fluttering like a little bird; and if you feel cold when night comes on, tell me, my Pierre, and I will wrap you in my cloak. Kiss your father, and ask his pardon for having been naughty. Say that it will never happen again, — never. Do you understand?"

"Yes, on condition that I always do as he likes, I suppose," said Germain, wiping the child's eyes with his handkerchief. " Ah, Marie, you will spoil that child ! I do not know why you did not come to us as shepherdess last St. John's Day. You could have taken care of my children, and I should have greatly preferred paying you a good price for serving them to going in search of a wife who may perhaps believe that she does me a great kindness in not detesting them."

" You must not look at things in the wrong way like that," replied little Marie, holding the horse's bridle while Germain placed his son upon the front of the large goat-skin-covered pack-saddle. " If your wife does not like children, you can take me into your service next year, and I will amuse them so well that they will never notice anything, you may be sure of that."

VII.

IN THE LANDE.

"WELL," said Germain, when they had gone a few steps, "what will they think at home when they do not see this little fellow return? The old people will be anxious, and will look for him everywhere."

"You can tell the laborer who is working up there on the road that you are taking him with you, and ask him to inform your people."

"True, Marie; you think of everything. I did not remember that Jeannie must be working there."

"And he lives quite near the farm; he will not fail to do your errand."

When they had attended to this precaution, Germain put the mare on a trot once more, and little Pierre was so joyful that he did not perceive at once that he had not dined; but the motion of the horse making his stomach feel empty, he began, at the end of a league, to yawn, to turn pale, and to admit that he was dying of hunger.

"Now it is beginning!" said Germain. "I knew very well that we should not go far without this gentleman's crying from hunger or thirst."

"I am thirsty too," said little Pierre.

"Well, shall we go into Mother Rebec's tavern at Corlay, the Point du Tour? It has a fine sign, but poor lodging. Come, Marie, you also will drink a drop of wine."

"No, no, I do not need anything. I will hold the mare while you go in with the child."

"But I remember, my good girl that this morning you gave the bread from your breakfast to my Pierre, and have eaten nothing; you would not dine with us, you did nothing but cry."

"Oh, I was not hungry, I was too unhappy; and I assure you that so far I have not had any desire to eat."

"You must force yourself to eat, my child; otherwise you will be ill. We have a long way to go, and we must not arrive there like starving people, asking for bread before saying good-day. I will set you the example myself, although I have not much appetite; but I shall succeed, considering that, after all, I have not dined either. I saw you and your mother crying, and that troubled my heart. Come, I will fasten the gray to the gate. Get down; I wish it."

They all three went into Mother Rebec's inn; and in a quarter of an hour the fat, lame hostess succeeded in serving them with an appetizing omelette, black bread, and some light wine.

Peasants do not eat fast, and little Pierre was so hungry that a good hour passed before Germain could think of setting out again. Little Marie had eaten out of complaisance at first; then, little by little, hunger had come, for at sixteen one cannot fast long, and country air is imperious. The kind words which Germain said to her to console her and to cause her to take courage also produced their effect. She made an effort to persuade herself that seven months would be quickly passed, and to think of the happiness which she would feel in finding herself again in her family and in her village, for Father Maurice and Germain agreed in promising to take her into their service. But as she was beginning to become cheerful and to jest with little Pierre, Germain conceived the unfortunate idea of making her look, through the inn window, at the fine view of the valley which can be seen in full from this height, and which is so smiling, green, and fertile. Marie looked, and asked if they could see the houses of Belair from there.

" Certainly," said Germain, " and the farm and even your house. Look! — that little gray point, not far from Godard's big poplar, lower than the belfry."

" Ah! I see it," said the girl; and with that she began to cry again.

" I was wrong to make you think of that," said Germain. " I can do nothing but stupid things to-day. Come, Marie, let us go, my child; the days are short, and in an hour, when the moon rises, it will not be warm."

They set out again and crossed the great heath; and as Germain, in order not to fatigue the young girl and the child by a too rapid pace, was unable to make the gray travel very fast, the sun had set when they left the road to enter the wood.

Germain knew the road as far as Magnier; but he thought that it would be shorter not to take the avenue to Chanteloube, but to go down by Presles and La Sépulture, — a direction which he was not accustomed to take when he went to the fair. He missed his way, and lost a little more time before he entered the wood; even then he did not go in on the right side, though he did not perceive it, so that he turned his back upon Fourche and went much higher up, toward D'Ardente.

What then prevented him from finding his way was a thick fog which came up with the night, — one of those autumn evening fogs which the whiteness of the moonlight makes still more vague and deceptive. The great pools of water with which the glades are strewn exhaled such thick vapors that when the gray passed through them they could be perceived only by the splashing of her feet and the difficulty with which she withdrew them from the mud.

When they had at last found a fine, straight alley, and when on arriving at the end of it Germain tried to see where he was, he discovered that he was lost; for Father

Maurice, in explaining the way to him, had told him that
on coming out of the wood he would have to go down a
very steep bit of hill, to pass through an immense meadow,
and to twice ford the river. He had even advised him to
enter the river carefully, because there had been heavy
rains at the beginning of the season, and the water might
be somewhat high. Seeing neither hill, meadow, nor river,
Germain stopped, looked for a house, waited for some
one to pass, and found nothing which could enlighten
him. Then he retraced his steps and entered the wood
again. But the fog grew thicker, the moon was completely hidden, the roads were frightful, and the ruts
deep. Twice the gray nearly fell. Loaded as she was,
she lost her courage; and even if she still preserved
enough sense not to run against trees, she could not prevent those who rode her from being troubled by large
branches which barred their way at the height of their
heads and placed them in great danger. Germain lost
his hat by a blow from one of these, and had great difficulty in finding it again. Little Pierre had gone to sleep,
and, lying as helpless as a sack, hampered his father's
arms so that he could neither guide the horse nor keep
her up.

"I believe that we are bewitched," said Germain, stop-
ping; "for this wood is not large enough for one to get
lost in it without being drunk, and here for two hours
at least we have been wandering about without being
able to get out. The mare has only one idea in her
head, which is to return to our house; and it is she who

made me lose my way. If we wished to go home, we need only let her have her own way. But when we are perhaps within a few steps of the place where we are to sleep, it would be foolish to give it up and make so long a journey over again. Still, I do not know what to do. I can see neither sky nor earth, and I am afraid that this child will catch the fever if we stay in this accursed fog, or that he may be crushed by our weight if the horse stumbles and falls."

"We ought not to keep on any longer," said little Marie. "Let us dismount, Germain. Give me the child; I can carry him very well, and I can prevent the cape from being displaced and leaving him uncovered better than you. You will lead the mare by the bridle, and perhaps we shall see more clearly when we are nearer the ground."

This expedient served only to save them from a fall from the horse, for the fog hung low and seemed to cling to the earth. Their progress was painful, and they were soon so exhausted that they stopped on finding a dry spot under the great oaks. Little Marie was in a violent perspiration, but she neither complained nor was anxious about anything. Wholly taken up with the child, she sat down upon the sand and laid him upon her knees, while Germain explored the neighborhood, after having passed the gray's reins over the branch of a tree.

But the latter, who was far from pleased with this journey, reared, loosened the reins, broke the girths, and giving half a dozen kicks higher than her head by way of receipt, set out through the underbrush, showing very clearly that she needed no one to find her way home for her.

"Well," said Germain, after having tried in vain to catch her, "here we are on foot, and it would be of no use for us to be in the right road, for we should have to ford the river; and seeing how full these roads are of water, we may be sure that the river has overflowed the meadow. We do not know the other roads, consequently we must wait until this fog lifts; it cannot last more than an hour or two. When we can see our way we will look for a house, the first we come to on the edge of the wood. But now we cannot leave here. There is a ditch, a lake, I do not know what, ahead of us; and I could not tell very well what there is behind either, for I do not understand from what direction we reached here."

VIII.

BENEATH THE GREAT OAKS.

"WELL, let us have patience, Germain," said Marie. "We are not very uncomfortable upon this little hillock. The rain does not come through the foliage of these great oaks, and we can light a fire, for I feel old stumps which will come up easily and which are dry enough to blaze. You have a light, Germain? You were smoking your pipe awhile ago."

"I had. My tinder-box was on the pack-saddle in my bag, with the game which I was taking to my wife that is to be; but the wretched mare has carried everything off, even my cloak, which she will lose or tear against the branches."

"Not at all, Germain; the pack-saddle, the cloak, and the bag are all there on the ground, at your feet. She broke the girths and threw everything down beside her when she started off."

"It is true, egad!" said the farmer; "and if we could find a little dead wood by feeling for it, we should succeed in drying and warming ourselves."

"That is not difficult," said Marie; "dead wood is crackling everywhere under our feet. But first give me the pack-saddle."

"What do you wish to do?"

"Make a bed for the child. No, not like that, — upside down; he will not roll about in the hollow, and it is still warm from the horse's back. Prop it up for me on each side with the stones which you see there."

"I do not see them at all; have you eyes like a cat's?"

"There, now it is done, Germain. Give me your cloak, that I may wrap up his little feet, and I will place my cape over his body. See if he is not as comfortable as he would be in his bed, and feel how warm he is!"

"It is true! You know how to take care of children, Marie."

"There needs no magic for that. Now look for your tinder-box in the bag, and I will arrange the wood."

"This wood will never catch fire; it is too damp."

"You are doubtful about everything, Germain! Do you not recollect when you were a shepherd and made great fires in the fields in the very midst of the rain?"

"Yes; that is the talent of children who herd sheep, but I began to drive oxen as soon as I could walk."

"That is why you have more strength in your arms than cleverness with your hands. There, the fire is laid: you will see whether it will not burn. Give me the light, and a handful of dry fern. That is right. Now, blow! You have not weak lungs?"

"Not that I know of," said Germain, blowing like a blacksmith's bellows. After a moment the flame shone out, emitted at first a red light, and at last rose in a bluish blaze beneath the foliage of the oaks, struggling against the fog, and little by little drying the atmosphere for ten feet around.

"Now I will sit down beside the child, so that no sparks may fall upon him," said the young girl. "Do you put on wood and keep the fire bright, Germain. We shall catch neither fever nor cold here, I will answer for that."

"Upon my word, you are a clever girl," said Germain, "and you know how to make a fire like a little witch. I feel quite revived, and my courage is coming back to me; for with my legs wet to the knees, and with the idea of remaining here until daybreak, I was in a very bad humor awhile ago."

"And when one is in a bad humor, one never thinks of anything," returned little Marie.

"And are you never in a bad humor?"

"Why, no, never! What is the use of it?"

"Oh! there is no use of it, certainly; but how can one help it, when one has troubles? And yet God knows that you have not lacked them, my poor child; for you have not always been happy."

" It is true; my poor mother and I have suffered. We have been unhappy, but we have never lost courage."

" I should not lose courage before any work, no matter how hard," said Germain; " but poverty would make me wretched, for I have never wanted for anything. My wife made me rich, and so I still am. I shall be, so long as I work at the farm, which will be always, I hope. But every one must have his own troubles. I suffered in another way."

" Yes, you lost your wife, and it was a great pity."

" Was it not?"

" Oh, I wept for her sincerely, Germain, for she was so good! Come, let us not speak of her, for I should weep again. All my sorrows seem to be coming back to me to-day."

" It is true that she was very fond of you, little Marie; she thought a great deal of you and your mother. What! are you weeping? Come, my child, I do not wish to weep myself — "

" And yet you are weeping, Germain, you are weeping too. What is there to be ashamed of in weeping for one's wife? Do not mind me; I share that sorrow with you."

" You have a good heart, Marie, and it does me good to weep with you. But put your feet close to the fire; your skirts are wet too, my poor girl! Here, I will take your place beside the child; do you warm yourself better than that."

"I am warm enough," said Marie; "and if you wish to sit down, take a corner of the cloak. I am very well off."

"The fact is that we are not badly off here," said Germain, sitting down quite close to her. "Only hunger makes me a little uncomfortable. It must be nine o'clock, and I have had so much trouble travelling in these bad roads that I feel quite weak. Are you not hungry too, Marie?"

"I? Not at all. I am not accustomed, like you, to four meals a day, and I have so often had to go to bed without supper that one time more does not astonish me much."

"Well, a woman like you is a convenient person; she does not cost a great deal," said Germain, smiling.

"I am not a woman," said Marie, innocently, without perceiving the turn which the farmer's ideas were taking. "Are you dreaming?"

"Yes, I believe that I am dreaming," replied Germain; "perhaps it is hunger which makes me wander."

"What a gourmand you are!" returned she, brightening a little in turn. "Well, if you cannot live five or six hours without eating, have you not game there in your bag, and fire with which to cook it?"

"The deuce! that is a good idea. But how about the present to my future father-in-law?"

"You have six partridges and a hare. I do not suppose that you need all that to satisfy your hunger."

"But if we cook a partridge here, without a spit or andirons, it will be a coal."

"Not at all," said little Marie. "I will undertake to cook it under the coals without a taste of smoke. Have you never caught larks in the fields, and cooked them between two stones? Ah! it is true; I forgot that you had never been a shepherd. Come, pluck this partridge! Not so hard; you will tear off its skin."

"You might pluck the other to show me how."

"Do you want to eat two? What an ogre! Come, there they are plucked; I will cook them."

"You would make a perfect *cantinière*, Marie; but unfortunately you have no canteen, and I shall be reduced to drinking the water of this pool."

"You would like some wine, would you not? Perhaps you want some coffee. You fancy yourself at the fair, in a booth! Call the inn-keeper — 'Some brandy for the farmer of Belair!'"

"Ah, little tease, you are making fun of me! Would you not drink some wine, if you had any?"

"I? I drank some with you this evening at Mother Rebec's for the second time in my life; but if you are very good, I will give you a bottle, almost full, and excellent at that."

"How, Marie? Really, you are a witch!"

"Were you not foolish enough to ask for two bottles of wine at Mother Rebec's? You drank one with your boy, and I scarcely took three drops of that which you placed before me. Still, you paid for them both without noticing it."

"Well?"

"Well, I put in my basket that which had not been drunk, because I thought that you or your child might be thirsty on the way; and there it is."

"You are the most thoughtful girl that I ever met. Just see! And yet the poor child was weeping when she left the inn; but it did not prevent her from thinking of others rather than of herself. Little Marie, the man who marries you will be no fool."

"I hope not, for I should not like a fool. Come, eat your partridges, they are cooked to a turn; and for lack of bread, you must be satisfied with chestnuts."

"And where the deuce did you get chestnuts too?"

"There is nothing astonishing in that! All the way along, I took them from the branches as I passed, and I filled my pockets with them."

"And are they cooked too?"

"Where would my wits have been if I had not put them in the fire as soon as it was lighted? We always do that in the pastures."

"Well, little Marie, we will sup together. I want to drink your health and wish you a good husband, — oh, such a one as you would wish for yourself! Tell me a little about him."

"I should find it very difficult, Germain, for I have not thought about it yet."

"What! not at all, never?" said Germain, beginning to eat with a laborer's appetite, but cutting off the best pieces to offer them to his companion, who refused persistently, and contented herself with a few chestnuts. "Tell me, little Marie," he went on, seeing that she never answered him, "have you not yet thought of marriage? You are old enough, however."

"Perhaps," said she; "but I am too poor. One must have at least three hundred francs to set up housekeeping, and I shall have to work five or six years to get them."

"Poor child! I wish Father Maurice would give me three hundred francs, that I might make you a present of them."

"Many thanks, Germain. But what would they say of me?"

"What would they say? Every one knows that I am old and cannot marry you. Therefore they would not suppose that I — that you — "

"I say, farmer! your child is waking up," said little Marie.

IX.

THE EVENING PRAYER.

LITTLE Pierre had sat up and was looking about him with a pensive expression.

"Ah! he always does that when he hears any one eating," said Germain. "The sound of a cannon would not wake him; but when people move their jaws about him, he opens his eyes at once."

"You must have been like that at his age," said little Marie, with a mischievous smile. "Come, my Pierre, are you looking for the tester of your bed? It is made of leaves this evening, my child; but your father is eating supper none the less. Will you have some with him? I did not eat your share; I suspected that you would claim it."

"Marie, I wish you to eat," cried the farmer. "I will not eat any more. I am a glutton, a brute. You deprive yourself for us, and it is not just. I am ashamed of it. Really, it takes away my appetite. I will not have my son eat supper if you do not sup."

"Let us alone," replied little Marie; "you have not the key of our appetites. Mine is closed to-day, but your Pierre's is open like that of a little wolf. There, just see how he goes at it! Oh, he will be a splendid laborer too!"

Indeed, Pierre quickly showed whose son he was; and scarcely awake, and understanding neither where he was nor how he had come there, he began to devour. Then, when he was no longer hungry, being excited, as is the case with children when their habits are broken in upon, he had more cleverness, more curiosity, and more reasoning power than usual. He made them explain to him where he was; and when he knew that he was in a wood, he was somewhat frightened.

"Are there any bad beasts in this wood?" he asked his father.

"No," said the farmer, "there are none. Do not be afraid!"

"Then you did not tell me the truth when you told me that if I were to go with you in the big woods the wolves would carry me off?"

"Will you hear how he reasons?" said Germain, embarrassed.

"He is right," replied little Marie; "you told him that.

He has a good memory; he recollects. But you must know, my Pierre, that your father always tells the truth. We passed through the big woods while you were asleep, and now we are in the little wood where there are no bad beasts."

" Are the little woods very far from the big ones?"

" Far enough; besides, wolves never come out of the big woods. And then, if they were to come here, your father would kill them."

" And you too, little Marie?"

" And we too; for you would help us, would you not, my Pierre? You are not afraid? You would beat them hard?"

" Oh, yes," said the child, proudly, taking a heroic attitude, " we would kill them."

" There is no one like you for talking to children," said Germain to Marie, " and for making them listen to reason. It is true that it is not long since you were a child yourself, and that you recollect what your mother said to you. I believe that the younger one is, the better one understands those who are young. I am greatly afraid that a woman of thirty who does not yet know what it is to be a mother, will have trouble in learning to prattle and reason with children."

" Why, Germain? I do not know why you have a bad idea of this woman; you will change it."

" The devil take the woman!" said Germain. " I wish I were coming away from there, never to return. What do I want with a wife whom I do not know?"

"Papa," said the child, "why is it that you are always talking of your wife to-day, when she is dead?"

"Alas! Then you have not forgotten your poor, dear mother?"

"No, for I saw her placed in a beautiful box of white wood, and my grandmother took me to her to kiss her and say good-by to her! She was so white and cold, and every evening my aunt makes me pray the good Lord that she may go and be warm with Him in heaven. Do you suppose that she is there now?"

"I hope so, my child; but you must always pray, for that shows your mother that you love her."

"I will say my prayer now," replied the child; "I did not think of saying it this evening. But I cannot say it by myself; I always forget a little of it. Marie must help me."

"Yes, my Pierre, I will help you," said the young girl; "come here and kneel by me."

The child knelt upon the young girl's skirt, clasped his little hands, and began to repeat his prayer, fervently and attentively at first, then more slowly and hesitatingly, and finally repeating word for word what little Marie dictated to him, when he reached the place where, as sleep overcame him every evening, he had never been able to learn it to the end. This time also the effort of attention and the monotony of his own voice produced their wonted effect. He pronounced the last syllables with difficulty, and only after having had them repeated three times; his head grew heavy, and dropped upon

Marie's breast; his hands relaxed, fell apart, and dropped open upon his knees. By the light of the camp-fire Germain looked at his little angel sleeping upon the heart of the young girl, who, supporting him in her arms and warming his blond locks with her pure breath, had also given herself up to a pious revery, and was praying silently for the soul of Catherine.

Germain was touched, and tried to find something to say to Marie to convey to her all the esteem and gratitude with which she inspired him, but could find nothing which would express his thoughts. He approached her to kiss his son, whom she still held pressed against her breast, and found it difficult to remove his lips from Pierre's brow.

"You kiss him too hard," said Marie, gently pushing away the farmer's head; "you will wake him. Let me put him back to bed, now that he has set out again for the dreams of paradise."

The child allowed Marie to lay him down; but as he stretched himself out upon the goat-skin of the saddle, he asked whether he was upon the gray. Then, opening his great blue eyes and holding them fixed toward the branches for a minute, he appeared to be dreaming while wide awake, or to be struck by an idea which had come into his mind, and which was taking shape there at the approach of sleep. "My little papa," said he, "if you wish to give me another mother, I want her to be Marie."

And without waiting for a reply he closed his eyes and fell asleep.

X.

IN SPITE OF THE COLD.

LITTLE Marie did not appear to pay any attention to the child's odd words except to regard them as a sign of friendship. She wrapped him up carefully, and stirred up the fire; and as the mist which lay sleeping upon the neighboring pool showed no signs of clearing away, she advised Germain to make himself comfortable beside the fire and to take a nap.

"I see that you are already becoming sleepy," she said, "for you no longer say a word, and you are looking at the coals just as your little boy did awhile ago. Come, go to sleep; I will watch over your child and you."

"It is you who shall sleep," replied the farmer, "and I will guard you both; for I never felt less like sleeping, — I have fifty ideas in my head."

"Fifty are a great many," said the young girl, with a somewhat mocking significance; "there are so many people who would be glad to have one."

"Well, if I have not fifty, I have at least one, which has not left me this last hour."

"And I will tell you what it is, as well as those which you had before it."

"Very well, tell me what it is, if you guess it, Marie, — tell it to me yourself; it will give me pleasure."

"An hour ago," she returned, "you had the idea that you would like to eat, and now you have the idea that you would like to go to sleep."

"Marie, I am only an ox-driver, but really you take me for an ox. You are a cruel girl, and I see that you do not want to talk to me. So go to sleep; that will be better than criticising a man who is not in the least gay."

"If you wish to talk, let us talk," said the young girl, half reclining beside the child and leaning her head against the saddle. "You are tormenting yourself, Germain, and in that you do not show much courage for a man. What should I say if I did not defend myself better against my own sorrows?"

"Yes, no doubt; and that is precisely what concerns me, my poor child! You are going to live far from your relatives, and in a wretched country of *landes* and swamps, where you will catch autumn fevers, where wool-bearing

animals do not prosper, — which always annoys a shepherdess who means well; finally, you will be among strangers
who may not be good to you, perhaps, who will not understand your worth. Really, it grieves me more than I can
tell you, and I should like to take you back to your mother
instead of going to Fourche."

"You speak with a great deal of kindness, but unreasonably, my poor Germain. One ought not to be cowardly
for one's friends; and instead of showing me the bad side
of my lot, you ought to show me the good one, as you
did when we took luncheon at Mother Rebec's."

"I can't help it; it seemed to me so then, and now it
seems to me otherwise. You would do better to look for
a husband."

"That cannot be, Germain, — I told you so; and as it
cannot be, I do not think of it."

"But suppose it were to happen? Perhaps, if you were
to tell me what kind of man you would like him to be,
I might succeed in imagining some one."

"To imagine is not to find. I do not imagine anything,
since it is useless."

"It would not occur to you to find a rich husband?"

"No, certainly not, since I am as poor as Job."

"But if he were moderately well off, it would not be unpleasant for you to be well lodged, well fed, well dressed,
and in a family of good people who would permit you to
help your mother."

"Oh! as for that, yes. My only wish is to help my
mother."

"And suppose such a man were to be found, even though he were not in his first youth, you would not be too particular."

"Ah! I beg your pardon, Germain. That is precisely the thing on which I should insist. I could not love an old man."

"An old man, no doubt; but a man of my age, for instance."

"Your age is old for me, Germain. I should prefer the age of Bastien, although Bastien is not so handsome a man as you."

"You would prefer Bastien the swine-herd," said Germain, irritated, — "a lad whose eyes are like those of the animals which he keeps?"

"I could accept the eyes, for the sake of his eighteen years."

Germain felt horribly jealous. "Come," said he, "I see that you are set on Bastien. It is a comical idea, nevertheless."

"Yes, it would be a comical idea," replied little Marie, with a peal of laughter, "and he would make a comical husband. One could make him believe whatever one chose. For instance, the other day I picked up a tomato in the curé's garden. I told him that it was a fine red apple, and he bit into it like a glutton. If you had seen what a face he made, — oh, dear! how ugly he was!"

"Then you do not like him, since you make fun of him?"

"That would be no reason. But I do not like him; he is brutal to his little sister, and he is dirty."

"Well, you do not feel a fancy for somebody else?"

"What difference does that make to you, Germain?"

"It makes no difference to me; it is only to make conversation. I see, my girl, that you already have a lover in your head."

"No, Germain, you are mistaken. I have none as yet; it may come later. But since I shall not marry until I have laid up something, I am destined to marry late, and an old man."

"Well, take an old man at once!"

"No, indeed! When I am no longer young, my husband's age will be a matter of indifference to me; at present it would not be so."

"I see clearly, Marie, that I do not please you; that is evident enough," said Germain, with annoyance, and without weighing his words.

Little Marie did not reply. Germain leaned toward her; she was asleep. She had fallen, overcome and as if stunned by sleep, like children who are already asleep though still babbling.

Germain was glad that she had not noticed his last words; he recognized the fact that they were not wise, and he turned away to divert himself and change the train of his thoughts.

But it was all in vain. He could neither go to sleep nor think of anything but what he had just said. He walked about the fire twenty times, went away, and came back; finally, feeling as agitated as if he had been eating gunpowder, he leaned against the tree which sheltered the two children and watched them sleep.

"I do not know how it is that I never perceived," he thought, "that this little Marie is the prettiest girl in the neighborhood. She has not much color, but her face is as fresh as a wild rose. What a charming mouth and what a dainty nose! She is not large for her age, but she is formed like a quail, and light as a finch. I do not know why they made such a fuss at home about a great, fat, red woman. My wife was thin and pale, rather, yet she pleased me above every one else. This child is delicate, but she is not unhealthy, and she is as pretty to look at as a white kid! And then what a sweet and good look she has! How one can read her good heart in her eyes, even when they are closed in sleep! As for cleverness, she has more than my dear Catherine had, it must be confessed, and one would not be bored with her. She is gay, good, industrious, loving, and amusing. I do not see what better one could wish.

"But why do I think of all that?" Germain went on, trying to look in another direction. "My father-in-law would not hear of it, and all the family would think me mad. Besides, she herself would not have me, the poor child! She thinks me too old, — she told me so. She is disinterested; she cares little for enduring still more poverty and discomfort, for wearing poor clothes and suffering from hunger for two or three months out of the year, so long as she can satisfy her heart some day and

give herself a husband who pleases her. She is right!
I would do the same in her place; and even now, if I
could follow my own will, instead of making a marriage
which does not attract me, I would choose a girl to my
taste."

The more Germain strove to reason and to calm himself, the less he succeeded. He went away twenty paces
to hide himself in the fog, and then suddenly found himself upon his knees beside the two sleeping children.
Once, even, he wished to kiss little Pierre, who had one
arm about Marie's neck; and he mistook so completely
that Marie, feeling a breath hot as fire run over her lips,
awoke and looked at him with a frightened expression,
not understanding at all what was going on within him.

"I did not see you at all, my poor children," said Germain, hastily drawing back. "I came near falling over
you and hurting you."

Marie was innocent enough to believe him, and went to
sleep again. Germain passed over to the other side of
the fire, and swore before God that he would not move
until she awoke. He kept his word, but it was not without difficulty. He thought that he should become mad.

At last, toward midnight, the fog lifted, and Germain
could see the stars shining through the trees. The moon
came out also from behind the vapor which covered it,
and began to strew its diamonds upon the damp earth.
The trunks of the oaks remained in majestic obscurity;
but a little farther off the white stems of the birches
seemed like a row of phantoms in their shrouds. The

fire was reflected in the pool; and the frogs, beginning to be accustomed to it, ventured a few shrill and timid notes. The angular branches of the old trees, rough with pale lichens, stretched out and crossed one another like great bony arms over the heads of our travellers. It was a beautiful spot, but so lonely and gloomy that Germain, tired of suffering in it, began to sing and to throw stones into the water to divert his mind from the frightful oppression of solitude. He also wished to waken little Marie; and when he saw her rise and look to see what time it was he proposed to her that they should set out again.

"In two hours," he said, "the approach of day will make the air so cold that we shall not be able to stand it, in spite of our fire. Now we can see to travel, and we shall certainly find a house where they will take us in, or at least some hay-loft where we can spend the rest of the night under shelter."

Marie had no will; and although she still had a great desire to sleep, she made ready to go with Germain.

He took his son in his arms without waking him, and wished Marie to come close to him, to cover herself with his cloak, since she would not take back her cape, which was wrapped about Pierre.

When he felt the young girl so near him, Germain, who had diverted his mind and become bright for a moment, began to lose his head again. Twice or three times he moved away from her abruptly and allowed her to walk alone. Then, seeing that she had difficulty in keeping up with him, he would wait for her, draw her sharply toward him, and press her so hard that she was astonished and even vexed without daring to say so.

As they did not at all know from what direction they had come, they could not tell that in which they were going; so they again traversed the whole wood, found themselves once more at the entrance to the barren *lande*, retraced their steps, and after having circled about and walked for a long while, perceived a light through the branches.

"Good! here is a house," said Germain; "and the people are already awake, since the fire is lighted. Is it so very late?"

But it was not a house; it was the camp-fire which they had covered over when they left, and which had been rekindled again by the breeze.

They had walked for two hours to find themselves again at the point from which they set out.

XI.

UNDER THE STARS.

"THIS time I give it up!" said Germain, stamping his foot. "We are certainly bewitched, and we shall not get away from here before daylight. This place must be under a spell."

"Come, come, let us not lose our tempers," said Marie, "and let us make the best of it. We will build a larger fire. The child is so well wrapped up that he is in no danger, and it will not kill us to spend a night out of doors. Where did you hide the pack-saddle, Germain? Among the thorns, stupid! It is a pleasant place to go after it!"

"Hold the child, take him, while I get his bed from the brush; I do not want you to scratch your hands."

" I have it; here is the saddle, and a few scratches are not sword-wounds," replied the plucky young girl.

She set about making a bed for little Pierre, who was so sound asleep that he had not perceived his new journey. Germain put so much wood on the fire that all the forest round shone with it; but Marie was utterly worn out, and although she made no complaint, could no longer support herself upon her feet. She was pale, and her teeth chattered with cold and weakness. Germain took her in his arms to warm her; and the anxiety, compassion, and irresistible impulse of tenderness which took possession of his heart quieted his senses. His tongue became unloosed as by a miracle, and all shame disappearing, he said, —

" Marie, you please me, and I am very unhappy at not pleasing you. If you would accept me for your husband, neither father-in-law nor family, neighbors nor advice, could keep me from giving myself to you. I know that you would make my children happy, that you would teach them to respect the memory of their mother; and my conscience being at rest, I could satisfy my heart. I have always liked you, and now I feel so much in love with you that if you were to ask me to do your will in everything all my life, I would swear it on the spot. Look, I beg you, at the great love which I have for you, and try to forget my age. Think that it is a false idea which those have who think that a man of thirty is old. Besides, I am only eight-and-twenty. A young girl fears that she will be criticised if she takes a man ten or twelve years older than herself, because it is not the custom with us; but I have heard that in other districts they do not consider that, — that on the contrary they prefer to give as a support to a young girl a staid man, of well-tried industry, rather than a youth who may go wrong, and instead of a good fellow, which they thought him, become a bad one. Besides, years do not always make age. That depends upon one's strength and health. When a man is worn out by too great labor and poverty or by a dissipated life, he is old before five-and-twenty; whereas I — But you are not listening to me, Marie."

"Yes, Germain, I hear you distinctly," replied little Marie; "but I was thinking of what my mother has always said to me, — that a woman of sixty is greatly to be pitied when her husband is seventy-two or seventy-five, and can no longer work to support her. He becomes infirm, and she has to take care of him at an age when she herself has great need of ease and rest. It is thus that people come to end their days in the poorhouse."

"Parents are right in saying that, I admit, Marie," replied Germain; "but still they sacrifice all the time of youth, which is the best, to foreseeing what will happen to one at the age when one is no longer good for anything, and when it makes little difference whether one ends in one way or another. But I am not in danger of dying of hunger in my old age. I am in a position to lay up something, since, living with my wife's family, I work a great deal and spend nothing. Besides, I shall love you so much, don't you see, that it will prevent me from growing old.

They say that when a man is happy, he remains young; and I feel that I am younger than Bastien for loving you. For he does not love you; he is too stupid, too childish to understand how pretty and good you are, and how formed to be tenderly cared for. Come, Marie, do not detest me; I am not a bad man. I made my Catherine happy; she said before God upon her death-bed that she had never received anything but kindness from me, and she urged me to marry again. It seems to me that her spirit spoke to her child this evening, as he was going to sleep. Did you not hear what he said? And how his little mouth quivered, as his eyes looked at something in the air which we could not see! He saw his mother, be sure of it; and it was she who caused him to say that he wanted you to replace her."

"Germain," replied Marie, greatly astonished and very thoughtful, "you speak kindly, and all that you say is true. I am sure that I should do well to love you if it did not displease your family too much; but what would you have me do? My heart does not speak for you. I like you greatly; but although your age does not make you ugly, it frightens me. I feel as though you were some one like my uncle or godfather; that I owe you respect, and that there would be times when you would treat me as a little girl rather than as your wife and your equal. Besides, my comrades might perhaps laugh at me; and although it is stupid to pay any attention to that, I believe that I should be ashamed and a little sad the day of my wedding."

"Those are childish reasons, Marie; you speak like a child!"

"Well, yes, I am a child," said she, "and it is for that reason that I am afraid of too sedate a man. You see yourself that I am too young for you, since you already reproach me with talking unreasonably! I cannot have more reason than befits my age."

"Good heavens! how much am I to be pitied for being so awkward, and for expressing so badly what I think!" cried Germain. "Marie, you do not love me, that is the truth; you think me too simple and too heavy. If you loved me a little, you would not see my faults so clearly. But you do not love me, that is all!"

"Well, it is not my fault," she replied. "I did my best as I listened to you; but the more I tried, the less I could convince myself that we ought to be husband and wife."

Germain did not reply. He rested his head upon both hands, and it was impossible for little Marie to know whether he was weeping, sulking, or asleep. She was a little anxious at seeing him so gloomy and at not being able to divine what was going on in his mind; but she did not dare to say anything more to him, and as she was too much astonished at what had just happened to wish to go to sleep again, she waited impatiently for day, keeping up the fire and watching over the child, which Germain appeared to have forgotten. Nevertheless, Germain was not asleep; he was not reflecting upon his lot, nor forming projects of courage or plans of seduction. He was suffering; he had a mountain of weariness upon his heart. He would have liked to be dead. It seemed as if everything must go wrong with him; and if he could have wept, he would not have made half-way work of it. But there was a little anger with himself mingled with his suffering, and he was choking without being able or willing to complain.

When day had come, and the sounds of the country told it to Germain, he took his face from his hands and rose. He saw that little Marie had not slept either, but he could find nothing to say to show his concern for her. He was altogether discouraged. He hid the pack-saddle once more in the thicket, took his bag upon his shoulder, and holding his son by the hand, said,—

" Now, Marie, we will try to finish our journey. Would you like to have me take you to Les Ormeaux?"

"We will go out of the wood together," she replied; "and when we know where we are, we will each go our own way."

Germain did not reply. He was hurt because the young girl did not ask him to take her as far as Les Ormeaux, and he did not perceive that he had offered to do so in a tone which provoked a refusal.

A wood-cutter whom they met when they had gone a couple of hundred yards put them in the right road, and told them that after passing the large meadow they had only to go, the one straight ahead, the other to the left, to reach their respective destinations, which were, for that matter, so near together that one could distinctly see the houses of Fourche from the farm of Les Ormeaux, and *vice versa*.

Then, when they had thanked the wood-cutter and gone on, the man called them back to ask them whether they had not lost a horse.

"I found a handsome gray mare in my courtyard," said he, "where a wolf, perhaps, compelled her to seek refuge. My dogs barked during the night, and at daybreak I saw the animal under my shed; she is still there. Go there, and if you recognize her, take her away."

Germain, having given a description of the gray, and being convinced that it was really she, started to go for his saddle. Then little Marie offered to take the child to Les Ormeaux, where he could come for it after he had made his appearance at Fourche.

"He is not very neat after the night which we have had," said she. "I will brush his clothes, wash his pretty face, and brush his hair; and when he is all fine and handsome again, you can present him to your new family."

"And how do you know that I wish to go to Fourche?" replied Germain, crossly. "Perhaps I shall not go at all."

"Yes, Germain, you ought to go there, you will go," returned the young girl.

"You are in great haste to have me married to some one else, that you may be sure that I shall not persecute you any more."

"Come, Germain, think no more of that. It is an idea which came to you in the night, because that disagreeable adventure somewhat disturbed your mind. But now reason must come back to you. I promise you to forget what you said to me, and never to speak of it to any one."

"Oh, speak of it, if you like! I am not accustomed to deny my words. What I said to you was true and honest, and I will not blush for it before any one."

"Yes; but if your wife knew that just as you arrived you had been thinking of some one else, it would not dispose her favorably toward you. Therefore pay attention to the words which you speak to me now; do not look at me like that before people, with a singular expression. Think of Father Maurice, who counts on your obedience, and who would be very angry with me if I were to turn you from doing his will. Goodday, Germain. I will take little Pierre, that you may be compelled to go to Fourche. I shall keep him as a hostage."

"Then you want to go with her?" said the farmer to his son, seeing that he clung to little Marie's hands and followed her resolutely.

"Yes, father," replied the child, who had listened and understood after his fashion what had just been said unguardedly before him. "I will go with my Marie. You will come for me when you are through getting married; but I want Marie to remain my little mother."

"There, you see that he wishes it!" said Germain to the young girl. "Listen, Pierre; I also wish her to be your mother, and always to stay with you. It is she who does not wish it. Try to have her grant you what she refuses me."

"Be easy, papa; I will make her say yes. Little Marie always does what I want."

He went off with the young girl. Germain remained alone, sadder, more irresolute than ever.

XII.

THE QUEEN OF THE VILLAGE.

HOWEVER, when Germain had removed the marks of travel from his dress and the trappings of his horse, when he had mounted the gray and the road to Fourche had been pointed out to him, he thought that it was impossible to draw back now, and that he must forget this night of agitation like a dangerous dream.

He found Father Léonard at the threshold of his white house, seated upon a handsome wooden bench painted a spinach-green. There were six stone steps before the door, which showed that the house had a cellar. The wall of the garden and of the hemp-yard was grouted with lime and sand. It was a handsome dwelling, and might almost have been mistaken for the house of a townsman.

The future father-in-law came to meet Germain, and after asking him for five minutes news of all his family, added the phrase consecrated to questioning politely those whom one meets about the object of their journey : "You have come for a little turn in our neighborhood?"

"I came to see you," replied the farmer, "and to make you this little present of game on the part of my father-in-law, and to say to you also, from him, that you must know with what intentions I have come to see you."

"Ah, ha!" said Father Léonard, laughing and tapping his ample belly, "I see, I understand, I have it." And he added, winking : "You will not be the only one to pay your compliments, young man. There are already three in the house who are waiting like you. I never send any one away, and I should be greatly embarrassed to give the preference to any one, for they are all good matches. Nevertheless, for the sake of Father Maurice, and of the quality of the lands which you farm, I should prefer it to be you. But my daughter is of age, and mistress of her own fortune; she will, therefore, do as she likes. Go in, make yourself known; I hope you may draw the prize."

"Excuse me, I beg your pardon," replied Germain, greatly surprised at finding himself with company where he had expected to be alone. "I did not know that your daughter was already provided with suitors, and I did not come to strive for her with others."

"If you thought that, because you were slow in coming," replied Father Léonard, without losing his good-humor, "my daughter would find herself deserted, you were greatly

mistaken, my lad. Catherine has that with which to attract husbands, and her only difficulty will be in choosing.
But go into the house, I say, and do not lose courage.
She is a woman who is worth the trouble of being striven
for." And pushing Germain by the shoulders with a rough
jollity, he cried, as he entered the house, " Come, Catherine, here is one more! "

This jovial but coarse manner of being presented to the
widow in the presence of her other admirers completed
the farmer's embarrassment and annoyance. He felt awkward, and remained several minutes without daring to raise
his eyes to the beauty and her court.

The Widow Guérin was well formed, and did not lack
freshness; but she had an expression of face and wore
a costume which displeased Germain at the outset. She
looked bold and self-satisfied, and her cap, trimmed with
a triple row of lace, her silk apron, and her fichu of black
tulle were little in harmony with the picture which he had
formed for himself of a serious and staid widow.

This display in dress and this bold air caused him to
think her old and ugly, though she was neither. He
thought that so pretty a costume and such playful manners would befit the age and the bright mind of little
Marie, but that this widow's jests were heavy and in
doubtful taste, and that she wore her fine garments without distinction.

The three suitors were seated at a table loaded with
wine and meat, which were there for their use all Sunday
morning; for Father Léonard was fond of making a dis-

play of his wealth, and the widow was not sorry, either, to show her fine china, and to keep a table like a landed proprietress. Germain, simple and confiding as he was, noticed these things with sufficient penetration, and for the first time in his life kept upon the defensive in drinking. Father Léonard had forced him to take his place with his rivals, and sitting down opposite him, treated him as well as he knew how, and conversed with him in preference to the others. The present of game, in spite of the inroads into it which Germain had made upon his own account, was still sufficiently ample to produce an effect. The widow appeared touched by it, and the suitors cast a contemptuous glance at it.

Germain felt ill at ease in this company, and did not eat heartily. Father Léonard rallied him upon it. "You are very gloomy," he said, "and you are neglecting your glass. You must not let love take away your appetite, for a fasting lover is not able to think of pretty speeches like one who has cleared up his ideas with a drop of wine." Germain was mortified that they should consider him already in love; and the affected air of the widow, who lowered her eyes with a smile, like a person sure of the state of affairs, gave him a desire to protest against his supposed conquest. But he feared to appear uncivil, smiled, and took patience.

The widow's admirers seemed to him three boors. They must have been very rich for her to admit their pretensions. One was more than forty, and almost as fat as Father Léonard; the second had only one eye, and drank

so much that he was stupid; the third was young and good-looking enough, but he wished to appear clever, and said such flat things that they were pitiful. Nevertheless, the widow laughed as though she had admired all these silly speeches, and in that gave no sign of good taste. Germain thought at first that she was smitten with the fellow; but he soon perceived that he was himself encouraged in a particular fashion, and that she wished him to commit himself further. This caused him to feel self-conscious and to appear colder and graver.

The hour for Mass approached, and they rose from table to go to it together. It was necessary to go as far as Mers, a good half-league from there; and Germain was so tired that he would have greatly liked to have the time to take a nap first; but he was not accustomed to miss Mass, and he set out with the others.

The road was full of people; and the widow walked with a proud air, escorted by her three suitors, leaning upon the arm now of one, now of another, and bridling and carrying her head in the air. She would have greatly liked to show off the fourth before the eyes of those who passed; but Germain thought it so ridiculous to be thus dragged in the train of a petticoat that he kept at a decent distance, talking to Father Léonard, and finding means to distract and occupy him sufficiently for them not to have the appearance of forming part of the band.

XIII.

THE MASTER.

WHEN they reached the village, the widow stopped to wait for them. She was resolved to make her entrance with all her train; but Germain, denying her this satisfaction, left Father Léonard, greeted several acquaintances, and entered the church by another door. The widow was annoyed at this.

After Mass, she showed herself in triumph everywhere upon the green where they were dancing, and opened the dance with her three lovers in succession. Germain watched her, and thought that she danced well, but affectedly.

"Well," said Léonard to him, clapping him on the shoulder, "are you not going to dance with my daughter? You are too timid!"

"I never dance, since my wife's death," replied the farmer.

"Well, as you are looking for another, your mourning is finished in your heart as well as in your dress."

"That is no reason, Father Léonard; besides, I think myself too old. I no longer care to dance."

"Listen to me!" said Léonard, drawing him to a retired spot; "you were annoyed when you came to my house by seeing the place already surrounded by besiegers, and I see that you are extremely proud; but this is not reasonable, my lad. My daughter is accustomed to being courted, especially during the two years since her period of mourning ended; and it is not her place to make advances to you."

"Your daughter has been ready to marry for two years, and has not yet been able to make up her mind?" said Germain.

"She does not wish to be in a hurry, and she is right. Although she has a light manner, and does not appear to you, perhaps, to reflect a great deal, she is a woman of much sense, and knows very well what she is about."

"It does not seem so to me," said Germain, ingenuously, "for she has three suitors in her train; and if she knew what she wanted, there would be at least two whom she would think out of place, and whom she would beg to remain at home."

"Why so? You do not understand at all, Germain. She will not have either the old one, the one-eyed man, or the young fellow, I am almost certain; but if she were to send them away, people would think that she wished to remain a widow, and no one else would come."

"Ah, yes, these serve as a signboard."

"Precisely. What is the harm, if it suits them?"

"Every one to his taste!" said Germain.

"I see that it would not be yours. But come, you can wait. Supposing that you are preferred, you might have the place left to yourself."

"Yes, supposing! And how long would one have to wait before knowing?"

"That depends upon you, I think,— whether you know how to speak and persuade. Thus far my daughter has understood very clearly that the best part of her life would be that which she spent in allowing herself to be courted, and she does not feel in haste to become the servant of one man, when she can command several. Therefore, so long as the game pleases her, she can amuse herself; but if you please her better than the game, the game can cease. You have only not to get angry. Come back every Sunday, dance with her, let her understand that you are an applicant; and if you are considered more amiable and better bred than the others, some fine day you will be told so, no doubt."

"I beg your pardon, Father Léonard. Your daughter has a right to do as she likes, and I have none to blame her. In her place, I should do otherwise; I should be more frank, and I should not cause men to lose their time. who doubtless have something better to do than to dance attendance upon a woman who is making sport of them. But if she finds amusement and happiness in that, it is none of my business. Only I must tell you one thing which it has been a little embarrassing for me to confess to you since this morning, as you began by making a mistake concerning my intentions, and you have not given me time to reply to you, so that you believe what is not true. You must know that I did not come here with the object of asking for your daughter in marriage, but with that of buying a pair of oxen which you wish to take to the fair next week, and which my father-in-law thinks will suit him."

" I understand, Germain," replied Léonard, very coolly; " you have changed your mind upon seeing my daughter with her lovers. That is as you like. It seems that what attracts some repels others, and you have the right to withdraw, since you have not yet declared yourself. If you wish seriously to buy my oxen, you can see them in the pasture; we will talk it over, and whether we make this bargain or not, you will come and dine with us before going home."

" I do not want you to trouble yourself," returned Germain. " You may have some business here; I am bored by watching people dance while I do nothing. I will go and see your oxen, and join you after a while at your house."

Thereupon Germain slipped away and went toward the meadows, where Léonard had, indeed, shown him some of his cattle. It was true that Father Maurice had to buy a pair; and Germain thought that if he were to bring back a handsome yoke of oxen for a moderate price, he would more readily obtain pardon for having wilfully failed in the object of his journey.

He walked quickly, and soon found himself but a short distance from Les Ormeaux. Then he felt a need of going to kiss his son, and even of seeing little Marie again, although he had lost the hope and driven away the idea of owing his happiness to her. All that he had just seen and heard,—this coquettish and vain woman; this father, at once crafty and short-sighted, who encouraged his daughter in habits of pride and insincerity; this luxury of towns, which seemed to him a degradation of the dignity of country manners; this time lost in idle and silly conversation; this home so different from his own, and above all that profound discomfort which the man of the fields experiences when he breaks away from his laborious habits,—all the weariness and confusion which he had suffered during the last few hours, gave Germain a desire to be again with his child and his little neighbor. Had he not been in love with the latter, he would still have sought her, in order to distract his mind and to enable his spirits to recover their ordinary condition.

But he looked in vain in the neighboring meadows; he could see there neither little Marie nor Pierre. And yet it was the hour when the shepherds were in the fields. There was a large flock in a pasture; he asked a boy who was keeping them, whether the sheep belonged to the farm of Les Ormeaux.

"Yes," said he.

"Are you the shepherd? Do boys keep sheep in your part of the country?"

"No. I am keeping them to-day because the shepherdess has gone home; she was ill."

"But have you not a new shepherdess, who came this morning?"

"Oh, yes; but she has already gone too."

"How, gone? Had she not a child with her?"

"Yes; a little boy, who cried. They went away together, after a couple of hours."

"Went away? Where?"

"Whence they came, apparently. I did not ask them."

"But why did they go away?" asked Germain, more and more uneasy.

"How should I know?"

"Could they not agree upon the wages? Yet these must have been settled in advance."

"I cannot tell you anything about it. I saw them come in and go out, that is all."

Germain went to the farm, and questioned the laborers. No one could explain the reason to him; but it was certain that after speaking to the farmer, the young girl had gone away, leading the child, who was crying.

"Can they have maltreated my son?" cried Germain, whose eyes began to blaze.

"It was your son? How came he to be with that young girl? Where do you come from, and what is your name?"

Germain, seeing that, according to the country custom,

they were about to reply to his questions by others, stamped impatiently and asked to speak to the master.

The master was not there; he was not accustomed to remain all day when he came to the farm. He had mounted his horse, and set out for another of his farms, though no one knew which of them.

"But at any rate," said Germain, feeling a lively anxiety, "can you not guess the reason why this young girl left?"

The laborer exchanged a strange smile with his wife, and replied that he knew nothing about it, — that it was none of his business. All that Germain could learn was that the young girl and the child had gone in the direction of Fourche. He hurried to Fourche; the widow and her lovers had not yet returned, nor had Father Léonard. The servant told him that a young girl and a child had come to ask for him, but that, not knowing them, she had not been willing to receive them, and had advised them to go to Mers.

"And why did you refuse to receive them?" asked Germain, angrily. "Are people so suspicious here that they will not open their doors to their neighbors?"

"Ah!" replied the servant, "in a rich house like this, it is right that one should keep a good watch. I answer for everything when the masters are absent, and I cannot open to every one who comes along."

"It is a mean custom," said Germain, "and I would rather be poor than live in fear like that. Good-by, girl! good-by to your wretched country!"

He inquired in the neighboring houses. They had seen the shepherdess and the child. As the boy had left Belair suddenly, without being dressed, with his somewhat torn blouse and his little lamb-skin over his shoulders; and as Marie also was always, for excellent reasons, very poorly clad, they had taken them for beggars, and had offered them bread. The young girl had accepted a piece for the child, who was hungry; then she had set out very quickly with him, and had entered the wood.

Germain reflected a moment, and then asked if the farmer from Les Ormeaux had not come to Fourche.

"Yes," they replied; "he passed on horseback a few moments after the young girl."

"Was he running after her?"

"Ah! then you know him?" said, with a laugh, the innkeeper of the place, to whom he was speaking. "Yes, certainly; he is a devil of a fellow for running after the girls. But I do not think that he caught this one; although, after all, if he had seen her—"

"That is enough, thank you!" And he flew rather than ran to Léonard's stable. He threw the pack-saddle upon the gray, leaped into it, and set out at full gallop in the direction of the wood of Chanteloupe.

His heart bounded with anxiety and rage; sweat streamed from his brow. He spurred the gray till the blood ran, though she, finding herself on the road to her stable, needed little urging to make haste.

XIV.

THE OLD WOMAN.

GERMAIN soon found himself back at the place beside
the pool where he had spent the night. The fire
was still smoking; an old woman was picking up the remains of the supply of dead wood which little Marie had
piled up there. Germain stopped to interrogate her. She
was deaf, and misunderstanding his questions, replied, —

"Yes, my lad, this is the Haunted Pool. It is a bad
spot, and one must not approach it without throwing in
three stones with the left hand, while making the sign of
the cross with the right; that drives away the spirits. Otherwise misfortunes happen to those who go round it."

"I am not speaking of that," said Germain, going close to her, and shouting at the top of his voice; "have you not seen a young girl with a child passing in the wood?"

"Yes," replied the old woman; "a little child was drowned in it."

Germain shuddered from head to foot; but happily the old woman added, —

"That was a long while ago; in memory of the accident, they set up a handsome cross here. But one night when there was a heavy storm, the bad spirits cast it into the water. You can still see the end of it. If any one had the misfortune to stop here at night, he would be very sure of never being able to leave before daybreak. He might walk and walk in vain; he could travel two hundred leagues in the wood, and always find himself again in the same place."

The husbandman's imagination was impressed in spite of him by what he heard; and the idea of the misfortune which must happen to him in order to prove completely the truth of the old woman's assertions took such possession of his mind that he felt cold all over. In despair of obtaining any further information, he remounted and began to ride through the wood, calling Pierre with all his might, and whistling, cracking his whip, and breaking the branches to fill the forest with the noise of his passage, then listening if any voice replied to him; but he heard only the bells of the cows scattered through the underbrush, and the wild cry of the swine fighting in the glades.

At last Germain heard the sound of a horse following in his track; and a man of middle age, dark, robust, clad half like a townsman, called to him to stop. Germain had never seen the farmer of Les Ormeaux; but an instinct of anger caused him to think at once that it was he. He turned about, and looking him over from head to foot, awaited what he had to say to him.

"Have you not seen a young girl of fifteen or sixteen, with a little boy, pass this way?" said the farmer, assuming an air of indifference, although he was visibly disturbed.

"And what do you want of her?" asked Germain, without seeking to disguise his anger.

"I might say to you that it is none of your business, my friend! But as I have no reasons for concealing it, I will tell you that she is a shepherdess whom I had engaged for the year without knowing her. When she arrived, she seemed to me too young and too weak for the work of the farm. I declined her services, but I wished to pay the cost of her little journey, and she went away angry while I had my back turned. She was in such a hurry that she even forgot part of her things and her purse, which does not contain much certainly, — probably a few sous. However, as I had to pass this way, I thought that I should meet her and give her what she had forgotten and what I owe her."

Germain's mind was too honest for him not to hesitate on hearing this story, if not very probable, at least possible. He fastened a penetrating look upon the farmer, who supported this examination with much impudence or innocence.

" I wish to clear the matter up," thought Germain ; and restraining his indignation, he said : " She is a girl from our place. I know her ; she must be about here. Let us go on together ; no doubt we shall find her."

" You are right," said the farmer ; " let us go on. And yet if we do not find her at the end of the avenue, I shall give it up, for I have to take the road to D'Ardente."

" Oh," thought the husbandman, " I shall not leave you, even though I have to search for twenty-four hours with you about the Haunted Pool."

"Wait a moment ! " said Germain, fixing his eyes upon a clump of broom which was shaking singularly. " Hillo ! hillo ! Little Pierre, is it you? "

The child, recognizing his father's voice, came bounding from the broom like a little deer ; but when he saw that his father was accompanied by the farmer, he stopped as if frightened, and remained uncertain.

" Come, my Pierre, come ! It is I," cried Germain, riding to him, and springing from his horse to take him in his arms. " And where is little Marie? "

" She is there, hiding, because she is afraid of that wicked black man, and so am I."

" Ah, be easy ; I am here. — Marie ! Marie ! It is I."

Marie crawled forward ; and when she saw Germain, whom the farmer was following closely, she ran to throw herself into his arms ; and clinging to him, like a daughter to her father, she said: "Ah! my brave Germain, you will defend me; I am not afraid with you."

Germain shuddered. He looked at Marie. She was pale, and her garments were torn by the thorns among which she had run, seeking the brake, like a fawn pursued by hunters; but there was neither shame nor despair in her face.

"Your master wishes to speak to you," said he, still watching her features.

"My master!" said she, proudly. "That man is not my master, and never will be! It is you, Germain, who are my master. I wish you to take me back with you; I will serve you for nothing."

The farmer had come forward, feigning a little impatience. "Here, my child!" said he, "you forgot something at our house which I am bringing to you."

"Not at all, sir," replied little Marie; "I have forgotten nothing, and I have nothing to ask of you."

"But listen to me," said the farmer; "I have something to say to you. Come, do not be afraid; only two words."

"You can say them aloud; I have no secrets with you."

"Come and take your money, at least."

"My money! You do not owe me anything, thank God!"

"I suspected as much," said Germain, in an undertone; "but never mind, Marie, listen to what he has to say to you, for I am curious to know it. Go up to his horse; I will not lose sight of you."

Marie made three steps towards the farmer, who said to her, bending over the pommel of his saddle and lowering his voice: "My child, here is a louis for you! You will say nothing, do you understand? I will say that I found you too weak for the work of our farm. And let us hear no more about it. I will go to your house some of these days; and if you have said nothing, I will give you something more. And then, if you are more reasonable, you have only to speak; I will take you back with me, or I will go and talk to you after dark in the meadows. What present do you wish me to bring you?"

"There, sir, is the present which I make you," replied little Marie, aloud, throwing his louis in his face, and somewhat roughly even. "I thank you greatly, and beg you, when you come our way again, to send me word. All the lads of my neighborhood will go to receive you; for with us, they are very fond of masters who wish to make love to poor girls! You will see, they will wait for you!"

"You are a liar and a silly tattler," said the farmer, angrily, raising his stick threateningly. "You would like to make people believe what is not true, but you will not get any money from me; we know girls of your kind!"

Marie drew back frightened; but Germain sprang to the bridle of the farmer's horse, and shaking it vigorously,

said: "I understand now! Dismount, my man, dismount, and let us have a talk!"

The farmer was not anxious to take up the quarrel. He spurred his horse to free himself, and attempted to strike the husbandman's hands with his stick, to make him let go; but Germain dodged the blow, and taking him by the leg, unseated him and caused him to fall upon the fern, where he threw him down, although the farmer had risen to his feet and defended himself lustily. When he held him beneath him, Germain said, —

"Coward! I could thrash you soundly if I wished. But I do not like to hurt any one; and besides, no correction would mend your conscience. However, you shall not stir from here until you have asked this young girl's pardon upon your knees."

The farmer, who was accustomed to affairs of this kind, tried to make a jest of the matter. He insisted that his fault was not so grave, since it consisted only in words, and that he was quite willing to ask pardon, on condition that he kissed the girl, that they should go and drink a bottle of wine at the inn, and that they should part good friends.

"You disgust me!" said Germain, thrusting the farmer's face against the ground, "and I wish to see your ugly look no longer. There! blush if you can, and try to take the *road of the insulted*[1] when you come our way."

[1] This is the road which turns off from the principal street at the entrance of villages, and runs around them on the outside. Persons who are afraid of receiving some deserved insult are supposed to take it to avoid being seen.

He picked up the farmer's holly-wood stick, broke it over his knee to show the strength of his hands, and threw the pieces disdainfully to a distance. Then, taking his son by one hand and little Marie by the other, he walked away, trembling with indignation.

XV.

THE RETURN TO THE FARM.

A T the end of a quarter of an hour they had crossed the heath. They were trotting, and the gray was whinnying at each familiar object. Little Pierre related to his father what he had been able to comprehend of what had happened.

"When we arrived," said he, "that man came to speak to my Marie in the sheep-fold, where we had gone at once to see the pretty sheep. I had gone up into the manger to play, and the man did not see me. Then he said good-morning to my Marie, and kissed her."

"You allowed yourself to be kissed, Marie?" said Germain, trembling with anger.

"I thought it was a civility, a custom of the place, just as at home the grandmother kisses the young girls who enter her service, to show them that she adopts them and will be to them like a mother."

"And then," went on little Pierre, who was proud of having an adventure to relate, "that man said something bad to you, something which you told me never to repeat and not to remember; so I forgot it quickly. Still, if my father wishes me to tell him what it was —"

"No, my Pierre, I do not wish to hear it, and I wish you never to recollect it."

"In that case I will forget it again," replied the child. "After that, the man appeared to get angry because Marie told him that she would go away. He told her that he would give her whatever she wanted, a hundred francs! And my Marie got angry too. Then he came toward her, as though to hurt her. I was frightened, and I ran to Marie, screaming. Then the man said, 'What is that? Where does that child come from? Turn him out!' And he raised his stick to strike me. But my Marie prevented him, and said to him, 'We will have a talk later, sir; I must take this child to Fourche now, and afterwards I will come back.' And as soon as he had gone out of the fold, my Marie said to me, 'Let us go, my Pierre, let us leave here quickly; for that is a bad man, and he will only hurt us.' Then we passed behind the barns, crossed a little meadow, and went to Fourche to find you. But you were not there, and they would not let us wait for you. And then that man, who had mounted his black horse, came after us, and we ran away farther, and at last we went to hide in the wood. But he came there also; and when we heard him coming, we hid ourselves. Then when he had passed, we began to run again, to make our way home; and finally you came, and found us; and that is how everything happened. Is it not true, my Marie, that I have forgotten nothing?"

"Yes, my Pierre, it is the truth. Now, Germain, you can bear witness for me, and you will say to every one at home that if I could not remain there, it was not for lack of courage or the desire to work."

"And I will beg you, Marie, to ask yourself whether, when it comes to defending a woman and punishing a scoundrel, a man of eight-and-twenty is too old. I should like to know whether Bastien, or any other pretty fellow, rich in his ten years less than mine, would not have been crushed by *that man*, as little Pierre says; what do you think of it?"

"I think, Germain, that you have rendered me a great service, and I shall thank you all my life."

"Is that all?"

"My papa," said the child, "I have not thought of saying to Marie what I promised you. I have not had time, but I will tell it to her at the house, and I will tell it to my grandmother also."

This promise made by his child set Germain to reflecting. He would be obliged now to have an explanation with his people, and in telling them what fault he had to find with the Widow Guérin, not to let them know what other ideas had disposed him to such clear-sightedness and severity. When one is happy and proud, it seems easy to have the courage to cause others to accept one's will; but to be rejected on the one hand and blamed on the other does not constitute an agreeable situation.

Happily, little Pierre was asleep when they reached the farm, and Germain laid him upon his bed without awaking him. Then he entered upon all the explanations which he was able to give. Father Maurice, seated upon his three-legged stool, listened to him gravely; and although he was disappointed with the result of this journey, when Germain, after relating the systematic coquetry of the widow, asked his father-in-law whether he had time to go on the fifty-two Sundays of the year to pay his court, with the risk of being dismissed in the end, the old man replied, bending his head in assent, "You are not wrong, Germain; that could not be." And afterwards, when Germain told how he had been obliged to bring back little Marie as quickly as possible, to save her from the insults and perhaps from the violence of the unworthy master, Father Maurice again assented with an inclination of his head, saying, "You were not wrong, Germain; you did as you should."

When Germain had finished his story and had given all his reasons, the father and mother-in-law heaved simultaneously a great sigh of resignation as they looked at one another. Then the head of the family rose, saying, "Well! God's will be done! Liking cannot be ordered."

"Come to supper, Germain," said the mother-in-law. "It is unfortunate that this could not have been better arranged;

but God did not wish it, apparently. We must look some-where else."

"Yes," added the old man; "as my wife says, we will look somewhere else."

There was no other sound in the house; and when the next day little Pierre rose with the larks at daybreak, be-ing no longer excited by the extraordinary events of the preceding days, he relapsed into the apathy of little peas-ants of his age, forgot all that had passed through his head, and thought only of playing with his brothers and pretending to be a man with the oxen and horses.

Germain tried to forget also, by devoting himself to work; but he became so sad and absent-minded that every one observed it. He did not speak to Marie, he did not even look at her; and yet if he had been asked in what meadow she was and by what road she had passed, there was no hour of the day when he could not have told it if he had been willing to reply. He had not ventured to ask his relatives to receive her at the farm during the winter, and yet he knew well that she must be suffering be-cause of her poverty. But she did not suffer; and Mother Guillette could never comprehend how her little supply of wood did not diminish, and how her shed came to be al-ways full in the morning, when she had left it almost empty at night. It was the same with the wheat and po-tatoes. Some one entered the garret-window, and emptied a sack upon the floor without leaving any trace. The old woman was at once uneasy and delighted; she bade her daughter not to speak about it, saying that if any one knew of the miracle which was being performed for her, they would take her for a sorceress. She thought, indeed, that the devil had a hand in it, but she was in no haste to quarrel with him by calling down the exorcisms of the curate upon her house; she said to herself that it would be time enough for that when Satan came to ask her for her soul in return for his benefactions.

Little Marie better understood the truth; but she did not dare to speak of it to Germain, for fear lest he should return to his idea of marriage, and she pretended not to perceive anything.

XVI.

MOTHER MAURICE.

ONE day Mother Maurice, finding herself alone in the orchard with Germain, said to him kindly: " My poor son-in-law, I think that you are not well. You do not eat so heartily as usual, you no longer laugh, and you talk less and less. Has some one in our house, or have we ourselves, without knowing or wishing it, given you pain ? "

" No, mother," replied Germain ; " you have always been as good to me as the mother who brought me into the world, and I should be ungrateful if I were to find fault with you or your husband, or any one else in the house."

"In that case, my child, your sorrow for your wife's death must be returning upon you. Instead of disappearing with time, your grief grows greater; and you absolutely must do what your father-in-law very wisely advised you, — marry again."

"Yes, mother, that would be my own idea also; but the women whom you have advised me to seek in marriage do not suit me. When I see them, instead of forgetting my Catherine, I think of her the more."

"Then, apparently, Germain, we have not understood your taste. You must help us, therefore, by telling us the truth. No doubt there is somewhere a woman who is made for you, for God never makes any one without reserving for him his happiness in another person. So if you know where to find this woman who is necessary to you, take her; and whether she be handsome or ugly, young or old, rich or poor, my husband and I are determined to give you our consent; for we are tired of seeing you sad, and we cannot live easily unless you are so."

"Mother, you are as good to me as the good Lord, and my father likewise," replied Germain; "but your compassion cannot cure my trouble, — the girl whom I would like will not have me."

"Is it because she is too young? It would be unreasonable for you to become attached to a young thing."

"Well, yes, good mother, I have been foolish enough to become attached to a young thing, and I blame myself for it. I have done my best not to think of her; but whether I am at work or resting, at Mass or in bed, with my children or with you, I am always thinking of her, I can think of nothing else."

"Then it is as though your fate had been decided? There is only one remedy for that: it is for this girl to change her mind and listen to you. Therefore I must look to the matter, and see whether it be possible. You must tell me where she is and what is her name."

"Alas! dear mother, I dare not," said Germain, "for you will laugh at me."

"I shall not laugh at you, Germain, because you are unhappy, and I do not wish to make you more so. It is not Fanchette?"

"No, mother, it is not she."

"Or Rosette?"

"No."

"Tell me, then; for I shall never get through, if I have to name all the girls in the neighborhood."

Germain hung his head, and could not make up his mind to reply.

"Well," said Mother Maurice, "I will let you alone for to-day, Germain; perhaps you may be more willing to confide in me to-morrow, or your sister-in-law may be more adroit in questioning you."

And she picked up her basket, to go and spread the linen upon the bushes.

Germain did as do children who yield when they see that people are no longer paying any attention to them. He went after his mother-in-law, and told her, trembling, that it was Guillette's little Marie.

Great was Mother Maurice's surprise; this was the last girl of whom she would have thought. But she had the delicacy not to show astonishment, and to make her comments to herself. Then, seeing that her silence was oppressing Germain, she held out to him her basket, saying: "Well, is that any reason why you should not help me with my work? Carry this load, and come and talk to me. Have you reflected carefully, Germain? Are you thoroughly resolved?"

"Alas! dear mother, that is not the thing to say. I should be resolved if I could succeed. But as I should not be listened to, I am resolved only to cure myself if I can."

"And if you cannot?"

"Everything has a limit, Mother Maurice. When a horse is too heavily laden, he falls; and when an ox has nothing to eat, he dies."

"That is to say, you will die if you do not succeed? God forbid, Germain! I do not like to have such a man as you say those things, for when he says them he thinks them. You are very brave, and weakness is dangerous in strong men. Come, you must hope. I cannot imagine that a poor girl, and one to whom you do great honor in asking for her, would be able to refuse you."

"Yet it is true, she does refuse me."

"And what reasons does she give you for it?"

"That you have always been good to her, that her family owes much to yours, and that she does not wish to displease you by causing me to miss a rich marriage."

"If she says that, she shows right feeling, and she does well. But by telling you that, Germain, she does not cure you, for she no doubt says to you that she loves you, and that she would marry you if we were willing?"

"That is the worst of it! She says that her heart is not inclined toward me."

"If she says what she does not think, in order the better to send you from her, she is a child who deserves to have us love her and pass over her youth for the sake of her great good sense."

"Yes?" said Germain, filled with a hope which he had not yet conceived; "it would be very good and very upright of her! But if she is so reasonable, I am afraid that it is because I displease her."

"Germain," said Mother Maurice, "you must promise me to remain quiet during the whole week, not to torment yourself, to eat, to sleep, and to be gay as of old. I will speak to my husband; and if I gain his consent, you will then know the girl's true feelings toward you."

Germain promised, and the week passed without a word from Father Maurice to him in private. Nor did he appear to suspect anything. The husbandman strove to seem calm, but he was paler and more anxious than ever.

XVII.

LITTLE MARIE.

AT last, on Sunday morning, as they were coming from
Mass, his mother-in-law asked him what encourage-
ment he had received from his love since the conversation in the orchard.

"Why, none at all," he replied. "I have not spoken
to her."

"How do you expect to persuade her, if you do not
speak to her?"

"I have never spoken to her but once," said Germain.
"It was when we went to Fourche together; and since
then I have never said a single word to her. Her re-

fusal pained me so much that I preferred not to hear her repeat that she did not love me."

"Well, my son, you must speak to her now; your father-in-law authorizes you to do it. Come, take courage, I tell you, and, if necessary, I bid you; for you cannot remain in this doubt."

Germain obeyed. He reached Guillette's with hanging head and dejected mien. Little Marie was alone by the fireside, so pensive that she did not hear Germain come in. When she saw him, she bounded upon her chair with surprise, and became quite red.

"Little Marie," he said to her, sitting down beside her, "I have come to make you uncomfortable and to bore you, I know very well; but *the man and woman at home* (thus designating, according to the custom, the heads of the family) wish me to speak to you, and to ask you to marry me. You do not wish to; I expect that."

"Germain," replied little Marie, "is it really certain that you love me?"

"It vexes you, I know, but it is not my fault. If you could change your mind, I should be too happy; but no doubt I do not deserve that. Come, look at me, Marie; am I so very frightful?"

"No, Germain," replied she, with a smile, "you are handsomer than I."

"Do not ridicule me; consider me indulgently. I have not yet lost a hair or a tooth. My eyes tell you that I love you; so look in my eyes. It is written there, and every girl knows how to read that writing."

Marie looked in Germain's eyes with her playful assurance; then suddenly she turned away her head and began to tremble.

"Ah! Good heavens! I frighten you," said Germain. "You look at me as though I were the farmer of Les Ormeaux. Do not fear me, I beg of you; it pains me too much. I will not say bad things to you; I will not kiss you against your will; and when you wish me to go, you need only point to the door. Come, must I go out to have you stop trembling?"

Marie held out her hand to the husbandman, but without turning her head, which hung toward the fire, and without saying a word.

"I understand," said Germain; "you pity me, for you are kind. You are sorry to make me unhappy; but still you cannot love me?"

"Why do you say such things to me, Germain?" replied Marie, at last. "Do you wish to make me cry?"

"Poor little girl, you have a good heart, I know; but you do not love me, and you hide your face from me that I may not see your dislike and repugnance. And I — I dare not even press your hand. In the wood, when my son was asleep and you were sleeping also, I came near kissing you very softly. But I would have died of shame rather than to ask it of you, and I suffered that night as much as a man burning in a slow fire. Since then I have dreamed of you every night. Ah, how I have kissed you, Marie! But you, during all that time, have slept without dreaming. And now, do you know what I think? It is that it you were to turn about and look at me with such an expression in your eyes as I have, I think I should fall dead for joy. And you think that if such a thing were to happen, you would die of anger and shame!"

Germain spoke as if in a dream, without hearing what he said. Little Marie was still trembling; but as he was trembling still more violently, he no longer perceived it. Suddenly she turned about; she was all in tears, and looked at him with an air of reproach. The poor husbandman thought that it was the last stroke, and without waiting for his sentence, rose to go; but the young girl stopped him by encircling him with her arms, and hiding her head in his breast, said, sobbing: "Ah, Germain, have you not guessed that I love you?"

Germain would have gone mad if his son, who was looking for him, and came into the cottage at full gallop upon a stick, with his little sister mounted behind him, and whipping this imaginary courser with a willow switch, had not recalled him to himself. He raised him in his arms, and placing him in those of his betrothed, said: "See! You have made more than one happy by loving me!"

APPENDIX.

———◆———

I.

A COUNTRY WEDDING.

HERE ends the story of Germain's marriage, as he told it to me himself. I ask your pardon, kind reader, for not having been able to translate it better; for it is a real translation that one must give of the old-fashioned and simple language of the peasants of the district which " I sing" (as they used to say). The speech of those people is too French for us; since the time of Rabelais and Montaigne the progress of the language has caused us to lose many old treasures. It is thus with all progress, and one must make the best of it. But it is still a pleasure to hear these picturesque idioms in use in the old territory of the centre of France, and all the more because they are the true expression of the mockingly tranquil and amusingly loquacious character of those who make use of them. Touraine has preserved a certain number of precious patriarchal locutions. But Touraine has become greatly civilized with and since the Renaissance. It has come to be covered with chateaux and roads, strangers and life. Berry has remained stationary, and I believe that after Brittany and a few provinces in the extreme south of France, it is the best *conserved* district which can be found at this day. Certain customs are so strange and curious that I hope to amuse you for a moment longer, dear reader, if you will allow me to relate to you in detail a country wedding — Germain's, for instance — at which I had the pleasure of being present a few years ago.

For everything, alas! is disappearing. During even my own lifetime there has been more progress in the ideas and customs of my village than had been seen during centuries before the Revolution. Already half of the Celtic, pagan, or Middle-Age ceremonies, which I saw in full force in my childhood, have vanished. A year or two more, perhaps, and the railways will pass their levels over our deep valleys, sweeping away, with the swiftness of lightning, our ancient traditions and our marvellous legends.

It was in winter, about Carnival time, — the period of the year when it is seemly and proper to have weddings with us. In summer there is scarcely leisure for it, for the farm-work cannot afford three days' delay, to say nothing of the additional days devoted to the more or less laborious digestion of the moral and physical intoxication caused by a fête. I was seated beneath the huge hood of an old-fashioned kitchen fireplace, when pistol-shots, the barking of dogs, and the shrill sound of bagpipes announced to me the approach of the betrothed couple. Soon Father and Mother Maurice, Germain and little Marie, followed by Jacques and his wife, the principal relatives on both sides, and the godfathers and godmothers of the betrothed entered the court-yard.

Marie, not having yet received the wedding presents termed *livrées*, was clad in the best her modest wardrobe afforded, — a gown of heavy dark cloth, a white fichu with large figures in striking colors, an apron of "*incarnat*" (a red cotton cloth, then much the fashion but now despised), and a muslin head-dress of dazzling whiteness, and of that happily preserved form which recalls the head-dresses of Anne Boleyn and Agnes Sorel. She was fresh and smiling and not at all proud, though she had good reason for it. Germain was grave and tender toward her, like young Jacob saluting Rachel beside Laban's well. Another girl would have assumed an air of importance and a triumphant bearing; for in every rank it is something to be married for one's good looks alone. But the young girl's eyes were misty and glittering with affection. One could see that she was deeply in love, and had no time to busy herself about the opinion of others. Her air of quiet resolution had not left her, but everything in her expressed kindness and good-will. There was nothing impertinent in her success, nothing personal in the consciousness of her strength. I never saw so charming a betrothed as she, when she replied frankly to her young girl friends, who asked her whether she was satisfied: " Ah, certainly I have no fault to find with the good Lord! "

Father Maurice was the spokesman; he came to pay the customary compliment and give the customary invitation. He first fastened to the hood of the fireplace a branch of laurel decorated with ribbons; this is called the *exploit*, — that is, the letter of notification. Then he distributed to each of those invited a little cross made of a bit of blue ribbon intersected by a bit of pink ribbon, — the pink for the fiancée, the blue for him who is to marry her; and those who are invited have to keep this cross to decorate with it, the women their head-dresses, the men their buttonholes, on the day of the wedding. It serves as a card of admission.

Then Father Maurice pronounced his compliment. He invited the master of the house and all his company — that is, all his children and relatives, friends and servants — to the benediction, the feast, the sports, the dance, and all that follows them. " I come to do you the honor of inviting you," — a very accurate expression, although it seems to us a contradiction, since it conveys the idea of doing honor to those who are held worthy of it.

In spite of the liberality of the invitation thus borne from house to house through the whole parish, politeness, which is very considerate among our peasants, prescribes that but two persons from each family shall take advantage of it, — one of the heads of the household, and one from the number of their children.

These invitations having been given, the betrothed couple and their families went to dine together at the farm.

Little Marie kept her three sheep upon the common, and Germain tilled the earth as if nothing had happened.

The day before that appointed for the wedding, about two in the afternoon, the music arrived, — that is, the players of the bagpipes and hurdy-gurdy, with their instruments decorated with long streamers of ribbon, and playing an appropriate march to a rhythm which would have been somewhat slow to feet not native to the soil, but perfectly harmonizing with the heavy nature of the ground and the hilly roads of the district. Pistol-shots, fired by young lads and boys, proclaimed the beginning of the wedding. The guests assembled gradually, and danced upon the turf before the house in order to get into the spirit of the occasion. When evening came they made strange preparations, dividing into two parties; and when night had set in they began the ceremony of the *livrées.*

This took place at the dwelling of the fiancée, Guillette's cottage. Guillette took with her her daughter, a dozen young and pretty shepherdesses, her daughter's friends and relatives, and two or three respectable matrons, — neighbors of decided character, prompt at repartee, and scrupulous guardians of the ancient customs. Then she chose a dozen vigorous champions, her friends and kinsfolk; and last of all the old hemp-dresser of the parish, — a voluble man and fine talker, if ever there was one.

The role which is played in Brittany by the *bazvalan,* the village tailor, is filled in our part of the country by the hemp-dresser and wool-carder, two professions often united in a single person. He is present at every ceremony, sad or gay, because he is essentially learned and a fine talker; and on these occasions he is always made spokesman, for the worthy accomplishment of certain formalities which have been in use from time immemorial. Strolling professions, which introduce a man into the bosom of families without permitting him to concentrate himself in his own, are apt to make him chatty and jocose, a story-teller and a singer.

The hemp-dresser is particularly sceptical. He and another rustic functionary, the grave-digger, of whom we shall speak in a moment, are the doubters of the neighborhood. They have talked of ghosts so much, and they know so well all the tricks of which these mischievous spirits are capable, that they have little fear of them. It is especially at night that they all — grave-digger, hemp-beaters, and ghosts — practise their trade. It is also at night that the hemp-beater narrates his mournful stories. Pray permit me to digress for a moment.

When the hemp has been properly prepared, that is, when it has been sufficiently soaked in running water and half dried upon the bank, it is brought back into the courts of the houses. It is placed upright in little sheaves which, with their stalks separated at the bottom and their heads tied in balls, bear no bad resemblance at night to a long procession of little white phantoms, standing on their slender legs and walking noiselessly beside the walls.

It is toward the end of September, when the nights are still warm, that they begin to beat hemp, by the pale light of the moon. During the day the hemp has been heated in an oven, from which it is withdrawn at night to be beaten hot. In this process they employ a kind of wooden horse surmounted by a lever which, falling in grooves, crushes the plant without cutting it. It is then that one hears at night in the country that sharp, crisp sound of three blows struck rapidly. Then there is a silence; the arm is withdrawing the handful of hemp to crush it upon another part of its length. Next the three blows are heard again; it is the other arm working the lever, and so on in the same way, until the moon is veiled by the first light of dawn. As this work lasts only during a few days of the year, the dogs cannot become accustomed to it, and send up plaintive howls toward every quarter of the horizon.

It is the season of strange and mysterious noises in the country. The migrating cranes pass at a height at which, in the daytime, the eye can scarcely distinguish them. At night one can only hear them; and these hoarse and mournful voices, lost in the clouds, seem the calls and the farewells of souls in torment which are striving to find the road to heaven, and which an inflexible fate compels to hover near the earth about the dwellings of men; for these migratory birds have strange uncertainties and mysterious anxieties in the course of their aerial journeys. They sometimes lose the wind, when capricious currents combat or follow each other in the higher regions. Then, when they are thus baffled during the daytime, one sees the file-leader floating aimlessly in the air, then turning about and coming to take his place at the tail of the triangular phalanx, while a skilful manœuvre of his companions quickly forms them in good order behind him. Often, after vain efforts, the exhausted guide gives up the attempt to lead the flight. Another presents himself, tries in turn, and yields up his place to a third, who recovers the current and triumphantly sets forward again. But what cries, reproaches, and remonstrances, what savage maledictions or anxious questions are exchanged in an unknown language between these winged pilgrims!

During the silent nights one can sometimes hear these gloomy noises circling for a long time over a house; and as one can see nothing, he feels, in spite of himself, a kind of fear and sympathetic uneasiness, until this sobbing flock has become lost in space.

There are still other sounds which are peculiar to this period of the year, and which are heard chiefly in orchards. The fruit is not yet gathered, and a thousand unwonted cracklings cause the trees to resemble animated beings. A branch creaks as it bends beneath a weight which has suddenly reached its extreme degree of development, or an apple drops and falls at your feet with a dull sound upon the damp earth. Then you can hear running away, as it rustles through the branches and grass, a being which you cannot see; it is the peasant's dog, — that curious, uneasy prowler, at once insolent and cowardly, which goes everywhere, never sleeps, is always seeking for one knows not what, spies upon you, concealed in the bushes, and takes to flight at the sound of the falling apple, thinking that you have thrown a stone at him.

It is during these misty, grayish nights that the hemp-dresser narrates his strange adventures with will-o'-the-wisps and white hares, of souls in torment and of sorcerers transformed into wolves, of the witches' Sabbath at the cross-roads and of prophetic owls in the graveyards. I recollect having spent in this way the first hours of the night beside the busy crushing-machines, the pitiless strokes of which, interrupting the hemp-dresser's story at the most terrible passage, would send a cold chill through our veins. And often, too, the good man would continue to talk while he beat the hemp, and there would be four or five words lost — terrible words, no doubt — which we dared not make him repeat, and the omission of which added a still more frightful mystery to the mysteries, already so terrible, of his story. It was in vain that the maids warned us that it was very late to remain out of doors, and that our bed-time had long since struck; they were themselves dying to hear more. And then with what terror did we traverse the hamlet on our way home! How deep did the church porch appear to us, and how thick and black the shadows of the old trees! As for the graveyard, we never saw it; we closed our eyes as we passed it.

But the hemp-dresser is not solely devoted, any more than the sacristan, to the pleasure of frightening people; he likes to make them laugh. He is a jester, and sentimental at a pinch, when it is necessary to sing love and marriage. It is he who collects and preserves in his memory the most ancient songs and transmits them to posterity. Consequently it is he who assumes at weddings the character which we are about to see him enact at the presentation of little Marie's *livrées*.

II.

THE LIVRÉES.

WHEN they were all assembled in the house, they closed the doors and windows with the utmost care; they even barricaded the window of the attic. They placed boards, benches, stumps, and tables across every entrance, as if preparing to resist a siege, and then there fell upon this fortified interior a solemn silence of expectation, until songs, laughter, and the sound of rustic musical instruments were heard in the distance. It was the bridegroom's band with Germain at its head, accompanied by his boldest companions, and the grave-digger by his kinsfolk, friends, and servants, who formed a gay and lusty party.

As they drew near the house they walked more slowly, consulted together, and became silent. The young girls, shut up in the building, had arranged little loop-holes at the windows through which they saw the men arrive and spread out in battle array. A fine, cold rain was falling, which added to the piquancy of the situation, since there was a great fire crackling upon the hearth of the house. Marie would have preferred to abridge the inevitable slowness of this regular siege; she did not like to see her betrothed cooling his heels in such a fashion, but she had no vote in the chapter in the circumstances, and she was even obliged to share ostensibly in the mischievous cruelty of her companions.

When the two armies were thus face to face, a discharge of arms by those outside set all the dogs in the neighborhood to baying. Those in the house sprang to the door barking, thinking the attack real; and the little children, whom their mothers strove in vain to reassure, began to cry and to tremble. This whole scene was so well played that a stranger would have been deceived by it and might perhaps have thought of putting himself in a condition of defence against a band of *chauffeurs.* Then the grave-digger, the bard and orator of the lover, took his place before the door, and in a doleful voice began the following conversation with the hemp-dresser, who was at a garret window above this same door: —

Grave-digger. Alas! my good people, my dear parishioners, for the love of heaven let us in.

Hemp-dresser. Who are you, and why do you take the

liberty of calling us your dear parishioners? We do not know you.

Grave-digger. We are honest folk, in great trouble. Do not be afraid of us, my friends! Show us hospitality. There is sleet falling; our poor feet are frozen, and we have come from so far that our sabots are split.

Hemp-dresser. If your sabots are split you can look upon the ground; you will certainly find a bit of willow with which to make *arcelets* (little curved bands of iron which are placed upon split sabots to strengthen them).

Grave-digger. Arcelets of willow are not very strong. You are mocking us, good people, and you would do better to let us in. We can see a fine fire blazing in your house; no doubt the spit is turning and one can enjoy himself with you, heart and stomach. So open to poor pilgrims, who will die at your door if you have not pity on them.

Hemp-dresser. Ah, ha! you are pilgrims? You did not tell us that. And from what pilgrimage are you returning, pray?

Grave-digger. We will tell you that when you have opened the door, for we have come from such a distance that you would not believe us.

Hemp-dresser. Open the door? Oh! by no means. We cannot trust you. Come; are you returning from Saint Sylvain de Pouligny?

Grave-digger. We have been to Saint Sylvain de Pouligny, but we have been much farther still.

Hemp-dresser. Have you been so far as Saint Solange?

Grave-digger. We have certainly been to Saint Solange; but we have been farther yet.

Hemp-dresser. That is not true; for you have never been even to Saint Solange.

Grave-digger. We have been farther, for we are just back from Saint James of Compostella.

Hemp-dresser. What nonsense are you telling us? We do not know that parish. We see clearly that you are bad men, robbers, good-for-nothings, and liars. Go somewhere else to tell your stories; we are upon our guard, and you shall not come in here.

Grave-digger. Alas! my poor man, have pity on us! We are not pilgrims, you guessed rightly; but we are unfortunate poachers pursued by the guards. The gendarmes likewise are after us, and if you do not hide us in your hay-loft, we shall be caught and taken to prison.

Hemp-dresser. And who will prove to us that this time you are what you say you are? For you have already told one lie which you could not maintain.

Grave-digger. If you will open to us, we will show you a fine piece of game which we have killed.

Hemp-dresser. Show it to us at once, for we do not trust you.

Grave-digger. Well, open a door or a window, that we may hand you the creature.

Hemp-dresser. Oh, by no means! Not so stupid! I am looking at you through a little crack, and I cannot see among you either a hunter or game.

Here an ox-driver, heavily built and of herculean strength,

came forward from the group in which he had stood unperceived and raised toward the window a plucked goose, stuck upon a strong iron spit, ornamented with bunches of straw and ribbons.

" Oh, ho ! " cried the hemp-dresser, after cautiously passing out an arm to feel the roast, "this is not a quail nor a partridge; it is neither a hare nor a rabbit; it is something like a goose or a turkey. Really, you are fine hunters, and that game has not made you travel far. Go somewhere else, you rascals ! We understand all your lies, and you may as well go home and cook your supper. You shall not eat ours."

Grave-digger. Alas ! Good Heavens, where shall we go to cook our game? It is very little for such a number as we are; and besides, we have neither a fire nor a place to go. At this hour every door is closed, every one is in bed; there is no one but you who has a feast in his house, and you must have a very hard heart to allow us to freeze outside. Once more, good people, let us in; we shall not cost you anything. You see that we bring the roast; only a little place at your fireside, only a little fire to cook it, and we shall go away satisfied.

Hemp-dresser. Do you think that there is too much room in our house, and that wood costs us nothing?

Grave-digger. We have here a little bunch of straw to make the fire; we will be satisfied with that. Give us but permission to put the spit across your fireplace.

Hemp-dresser. That cannot be; you fill us with disgust, not with pity. My opinion is that you are drunk, that you need nothing, and that you wish to come into our house to rob us of our fire and our girls.

Grave-digger. Since you will not listen to any good reason, we will get in by force.

Hemp-dresser. Try it, if you like. We are barricaded well enough not to fear you. And since you are insolent, we will reply to you no longer.

Thereupon the hemp-dresser closed the garret window with a great noise, and came down into the room beneath by a ladder. Then he took the bride by the hand, and the young people of both sexes joining them, they all began to dance and shout gayly, while the matrons sang in a piercing voice, and uttered great bursts of laughter in sign of contempt and of bravado against those outside who were attempting the assault.

The besiegers, on their side, made a terrible uproar. They fired their pistols against the doors, caused the dogs to bark, beat violently upon the walls, shook the shutters, and uttered frightful cries. In short, they made such a noise that one could not hear, and such dust and smoke that one could not see.

This attack, however, was only a pretence; the moment had not arrived for breaking through etiquette. If they succeeded, as they prowled round the house, in finding an unguarded passage or an opening of any kind, they might attempt to enter by surprise; and then, if he who carried the spit succeeded in placing his roast upon the fire, the capture of the fireplace being thus proven, the comedy ended and the lover conquered.

But the entrances to the house were not sufficiently numerous for the customary precautions to have been neglected, and no one would have assumed the right to use violence before the moment fixed for the struggle.

When they were tired of leaping about and shouting, the hemp-dresser began to think of capitulating. He went back to his window, and greeted the disappointed besiegers with a burst of laughter.

"Well, my lads," said he, "you are finely beaten! You thought that nothing was easier than to enter here, and you see that our defence is good. But we are beginning to feel pity for you, if you will submit and accept our conditions."

Grave-digger. Speak, good people; tell us what we must do in order to come in to your fire.

Hemp-dresser. You must sing, my friends, but a song which we do not know, and to which we cannot reply by a better.

"That will be easy enough," replied the grave-digger, and he began in a loud voice, —

"Six months ago 't was springtime —"

"I wandered o'er the new-sprung grass,"

replied the hemp-dresser, in a somewhat hoarse but terrible voice. "Are you mocking us, my poor fellows, that you sing us such antiquities? You see that we can stop you at the first words."

The grave-digger continued, —

"It was a prince's daughter —"

"And she would fain be wed,"

replied the hemp-dresser. "Go on to another! We know that a little too well."

"How do you like this?" said the grave-digger, —

"As I came back from Nantes —"

"I was all a-weary,"

replied the hemp-dresser. "That was sung in my grand-mother's time. Try another."

"As I walked out one morning —"

sang the grave-digger.

"Beside this charming wood!"

replied the hemp-dresser. "That is a fine one! Our little children would not give themselves the trouble to reply to you. What! Is that all you know?"

"Oh, we will sing you so many that at last you will be at a loss," replied the grave-digger.

A good hour was spent in this contest. As the two antagonists were the most learned persons in the neighborhood in the matter of songs, and as their repertory appeared inexhaustible, it might have lasted all night, especially as the hemp-dresser was malicious enough to allow them to sing certain complaints of ten, twenty, or thirty verses, pretending, by his silence, to confess himself conquered. Then they triumphed in the lover's camp, singing in chorus at the top of their voices, and believing that this time the opposing party would fail; but half way through the last verse they would hear the rough, hoarse voice of the old hemp-dresser shouting the concluding words, after which he would cry: "You need not have tired yourselves by singing so long an one, my children; we had it at our fingers' ends!"

Once or twice, however, the hemp-dresser made a grimace, frowned, and turned with a disappointed expression toward the attentive matrons. The grave-digger was singing something so old that his adversary had forgotten it, or had perhaps never known it; but immediately the old women would bawl out, in tones as sharp as those of gulls, the conquering refrain, and the grave-digger, compelled to surrender, would pass on to a fresh attempt.

It would have taken too long to wait to see which side would gain the victory. Marie's party declared that it would grant Germain's followers mercy on condition that they would offer her a present worthy of her.

Then began the song of the *livrées*, to a tune as solemn as a church air.

The men outside sang in unison in the bass: —

> "Hasten, Marie, hasten,
>   And open now thy door;
> For thee I've wedding gifts in store,
>   Have pity, love, unclose thy door."

To which the women replied in falsetto, from within, in a plaintive tone: —

> "My father is sad, and my mother mourns,
>   Through all the long and weary night,
> And I am a maid of too much grace,
>   To open ere morning light."

The men repeated the first verse as far as the fourth line, which they thus modified: —

> "Of kerchiefs fine we have a store."

But in the name of the fiancee, the women replied as they did the first time.

Through twenty verses at least the men enumerated all the gifts in the *livrée*, always mentioning a new article in the last line, — a handsome apron, beautiful ribbons, a cloth gown, lace, a cross of gold, and even a hundred pins to complete the bride's modest trousseau. The refusal of the matrons was irrevocable; but at last the bachelors decided to speak of *a handsome husband* which they had for her, and they replied, addressing the bride and singing to her with the men: —

> " Hasten, Marie, hasten,
>   And open now thy door.
> A husband waits; resist no more,
>   But let him pass thy threshold o'er."

III.

THE WEDDING.

THE hemp-dresser immediately removed the wooden bar which closed the door inside, and which was still, at that period, the only lock known in the greater part of the houses in our village. The bridegroom's band burst into the bride's dwelling, but not without a struggle; for the young men stationed in the house, and even the old hemp-dresser and the matrons, strove to guard the fireplace. He who carried the spit, supported by his party, had to succeed in placing the roast on the fire. It was a veritable battle, although they refrained from blows and although there was no anger in this strife. But they pushed and pressed so straitly upon one another, and there was so much vanity felt in this trial of muscular strength, that the results might have been more serious than they appeared amid the laughter and songs. The poor old hemp-dresser, who fought like a lion, was pushed against the wall and so crushed by the crowd that he lost his breath. More than one champion was overthrown and involuntarily trodden under foot; more than one hand which grasped the spit was covered with blood. These sports are dangerous, and the accidents have been sufficiently grave of late to cause our peasants to allow the ceremony of the *livrées* to fall into disuse. I think that we saw the last at the wedding of Françoise Meillant, and that combat was only feigned.

This struggle was still sufficiently earnest at Germain's wedding. It was a point of honor on one side to capture, on the other to defend, Guillette's fireplace. The enormous iron spit was twisted like a screw by the vigorous hands which fought for it. A pistol-shot set fire to a little supply of hemp in sheaves which lay upon a shelf near the ceiling. This incident caused a diversion, and while some hastened to extinguish this germ of a fire, the grave-digger, who had climbed into the garret without being perceived, came down by the chimney and grasped the spit, as the ox-herd, who was defending it near the fireplace, had raised it above his head to prevent its being torn from him. Some time before the capture by assault, the matrons had taken the precaution to put out the fire, for fear that in struggling near it some one might fall into

it and be burned. The facetious grave-digger, who had
concerted with the ox-herd, consequently obtained possession of the trophy without difficulty, and threw it across
the andirons. It was done! No one was now allowed to
touch it. He sprang into the middle of the room and set
fire to a remnant of straw about the spit, to make a pretence of cooking the roast, for the goose was in pieces
and strewed the floor with its scattered members.

Then there were much laughter and many boastful dis-
cussions. Every one showed the bruises which he had
received, and as it was often the hand of a friend which
had given the blow, no one complained or was angry.
The hemp-dresser, half flattened out, rubbed his back,
saying that he cared very little, but that he protested
against the stratagem of his friend the grave-digger, and
that if he had not been half-dead, the fireplace would not
have been won so easily. The matrons swept up the
floor, and quiet was restored. The table was covered
with jugs of new wine. When they had drunk together
and recovered their breath, the bridegroom was led into
the middle of the room, and, armed with a wand, was
subjected to a new ordeal.

During the struggle the bride had been hidden with
three of her companions by her mother, her godmother,
and her aunts, who had caused the four young girls to
sit down upon a bench in a retired corner of the room,
and had covered them with a large white cloth. The
three companions had been chosen of the same size as
Marie, and their head-dresses were of the same height;

so that as the cloth covered them from head to foot, it was impossible to distinguish one from another.

The bridegroom could not touch them save with the end of his switch, and then only to point out the one whom he believed to be his wife. They gave him time to examine, but only with his eyes; and the matrons, placed by his side, watched carefully that there was no cheating. If he made a mistake, he could not dance with his bride during the evening, but only with her whom he had chosen in error.

Germain, finding himself before these phantoms wrapped in the same shroud, was in great fear of making a mistake; and, indeed, that had happened to many another, for the precautions were always taken with scrupulous care. His heart beat. Little Marie did indeed try to breathe hard and to shake the cloth a little, but her mischievous rivals did the same, and there were as many mysterious signs as there were young girls beneath the veil. The square head-dresses supported this covering so evenly that it was impossible to see the form of a forehead outlined by its folds.

Germain, after hesitating ten minutes, closed his eyes, commended his soul to God, and stretched out the wand at random. It touched Marie's brow, and she threw the cloth from her with a cry of victory. Now he was at liberty to kiss her, and lifting her in his strong arms, he carried her into the middle of the room, and together they opened the ball, which lasted until two in the morning.

Then they separated to assemble again at eight o'clock.

As a certain number of young people had come from the neighboring villages, and as there were not enough beds for every one, each girl guest from the village received into her bed two or three young companions, while the lads went to stretch themselves out indiscriminately upon the hay in the farm loft. You can easily imagine that they did not sleep much, for they thought only of teasing one another, of cracking jokes, and of telling droll stories. At weddings three sleepless nights are the correct thing, and no one regrets them.

At the hour set for the departure, after they had eaten the milk soup, seasoned with a strong dash of pepper, to revive their appetites, — for the wedding feast promised to be abundant, — they reassembled in the courtyard of the farm. Our parish being suppressed, we had to go half a league away for the nuptial benediction. It was fine, cool weather; but as the roads were very bad, every one had provided himself with a horse, and each man took a young or an old companion behind him. Germain set out on the gray, which, well groomed, newly shod and decorated with ribbons, curvetted and breathed fire from her nostrils. He went to seek his bride at the cottage, with his brother-in-law Jacques, who, mounted upon the old gray, took good Mother Guillette behind him, while Germain returned to the courtyard of the farm, bringing his dear little wife with an air of triumph.

Then the gay cavalcade set out, escorted by the children, who walked, firing pistols and setting the horses to prancing. Mother Maurice was in a little cart with

Germain's three children and the musicians. They led the way, to the sound of the instruments. Pierre was so handsome that his old grandmother was very proud of him. But the impetuous child did not long remain with her. At a halt which they were obliged to make on coming to a difficult bit of road, he slipped away, and went to beg his father to take him before him on the gray.

"Oh," replied Germain, "that will bring down on us unpleasant jokes! It will never do."

"I care little for what the people of Saint Chartier may say," said little Marie. "Take him, Germain, I beg you; I shall be prouder of him than of my wedding-dress, even."

Germain yielded, and the handsome trio dashed through the ranks, the gray galloping triumphantly.

And indeed the people of Saint Chartier, although very sarcastic and somewhat teasing as regarded the people of the neighboring parishes which were joined to their own, never thought of laughing when they saw so handsome a groom, so pretty a bride, and a child whom a queen might have coveted. Pierre had a coat of bright blue, and a red waistcoat, so dainty and so short that it hardly descended below his chin. The village tailor had made it so tight that he could not make his little arms meet. And consequently how proud he was! He wore a round hat with a black and gold band, and a peacock feather rising saucily from a bunch of heron plumes. A bouquet of flowers larger than his head covered his shoulder, and the ribbons fluttered to his feet. The hemp-dresser, who was likewise the barber and hairdresser of the place, had cut his hair round, by covering his head with a bowl and clipping off whatever fell below it, — an infallible method for guiding the scissors. Accoutred in this way, the poor child was assuredly less poetic than with his flowing locks and his sheep-skin, like Saint John Baptist; but he did not think so, and every one admired him, saying that he looked like a little man. His beauty triumphed over everything; indeed, what is there over which the incomparable beauty of childhood would not triumph?

His little sister Solange wore for the first time in her life a head-dress in place of the hood which little girls wear until they are two or three years old. And what a head-dress! — taller and broader than the poor child's whole body. And how fine she thought herself for it! She did not dare to turn her head, and sat stiffly upright, thinking that she would be taken for the bride.

As for little Sylvain, he was still in a frock; and, asleep on his grandmother's knee, little knew what a wedding is.

Germain looked lovingly at his children; and when he came to the mayor's office, said to his betrothed, —

"Ah, Marie, I reach here a little happier than the day I brought you home from the wood of Chanteloube, thinking that you would never love me. I took you in my arms to lift you down as I do now, but I thought that never again should we be upon this good gray, with this child upon our knees. Do you know, I love you so dearly, I so love these poor children, I am so happy that you love me, and that you love them, and that my family love you, and I so love your mother and my friends and every one to-day, that I should need to have three or four hearts to suffice for it. Really, one is too small to contain so much friendship and so much happiness!"

There were crowds at the mayor's office and the church to look at the pretty bride. Why should we not describe her costume? It became her so well! The head-dress of white muslin, embroidered all over, was trimmed with lace. In those days peasants did not permit themselves to show a single lock; and although they conceal beneath their head-dresses magnificent hair rolled in white tape to support the head-dress, it would still be to-day an indecent and shameful action to show themselves bare-headed to men. Yet now they allow a narrow band to appear over their brows, and this improves them much. But I sigh for the classical head-dress of my own time. That white lace against the skin had a character of antique chastity which seemed to me more solemn; and when a face was beautiful thus, it was with a beauty the charm and simple majesty of which no words can describe.

Marie wore this head-dress, and her brow was so white and pure that the whiteness of the linen could not dim it. Although she had not closed her eyes the night before, the morning air, and above all the inward joy of a soul as transparent as the sky, as well as a secret flame, re-strained by the modesty of adolescence, gave her cheeks a glow as soft as a peach-blossom in the first rays of an April sun.

The white fichu, chastely crossed upon her breast, revealed only the delicate outline of a neck round as that of a turtle-dove. Her gown of fine myrtle-green cloth displayed her small figure, which seemed perfect, but which would still grow and develop, for she was not yet seventeen. She wore an apron of violet silk with the bib, which our villagers have unwisely abandoned, and which gave such elegance and modesty to the breast. Now they display their fichu with more pride; but there is no longer in their dress that fine flower of antique chastity which caused them to resemble Holbein's Virgins. They are more coquettish and graceful. The good form of former times was a kind of severe stiffness which made their rare smiles more profound and more ideal.

At the offertory Germain placed, according to the custom, the *treizain* — that is to say, thirteen pieces of silver — in the hand of his betrothed. He put upon her finger a silver ring, of a form which had not been varied for centuries, but which has since been replaced by the gold wedding-ring. As they left the church, Marie said in a low tone: "Is it the ring which I wished; that for which I asked you, Germain?"

"Yes," he replied, "that which my Catherine had upon her finger when she died. It was the same ring for my two marriages."

"Thank you, Germain," said the young girl, in a serious tone full of emotion; "I shall die with it, and if that be before you, you will keep it for the marriage of your little Solange."

IV.

THE CABBAGE.

THE wedding party remounted their horses and came back quickly to Belair. The feast was splendid, and, interspersed with songs and dances, lasted until midnight. The elders did not leave the table for fourteen hours. The grave-digger did the cooking, and very well he did it. He was famous for that, and he would leave his ovens to come and see them singing and dancing between each course. Yet this poor Father Bontemps was an epileptic! Who would have suspected it? He was as fresh, strong, and gay as a young man. One day we found him as if dead, contorted by his disease, in a ditch at nightfall. We took him to our house in a wheelbarrow, and spent the night in nursing him. Three days later he was at a wedding, where he sang like a thrush and leaped like a kid, frisking about after the ancient fashion. On leaving a wedding he would go to dig a grave and nail down a coffin, and although it would not appear afterwards in his gay manner, he would retain a gloomy impression which hastened the return of his attacks. His wife, a paralytic, had not moved from her chair for twenty years. His mother is a hundred and four, and is still living. But he, poor man, was killed last year by falling from his loft into the street. He was, no doubt, suffering from an attack of his disease, and, as was his custom, had hidden himself in the hay to avoid frightening and afflicting his family. He thus closed, in a tragic fashion, a life as strange as himself, — a mixture of events mournful and ludicrous, terrible and amusing, amid which his heart had always remained good and his character amiable.

But we have reached the third day of the wedding, which is the most curious, and is preserved in its integrity to our own time. We will not speak of the roast which is carried to the nuptial couch; it is a stupid custom which causes the bride's modesty to suffer, and tends to destroy that of the young girls who take part in it. Besides, I believe that the custom is in force in every province, and has no peculiar features with us.

Just as the ceremony of the *livrées* is the symbol of the taking possession of the heart and the house of the bride, that of the cabbage is emblematic of the fertility of the marriage. After breakfast on the day after the wedding comes this strange performance of Gallic origin, but which, modified by primitive Christianity, has become little by little a kind of " mystery," or Middle-Age moral buffoonery.

Two youths (the most amusing and best fitted of the band) disappear during breakfast, go and dress themselves, and finally reappear accompanied by musicians, dogs, children, and pistol-shots. They represent a couple of beggars, husband and wife, clad in the most wretched rags. The husband is the dirtier of the two; it is vice which has thus degraded him. The wife is only unhappy and debased by the misconduct of her husband.

They are called the *gardener* and his wife, and pretend to be charged with the care and culture of the sacred cabbage. But the husband bears different names which have each a meaning. He is termed the *pailloux*, because he wears a wig of straw or flax, and because, in order to conceal his nakedness, ill protected by his rags, he winds his legs and part of his body in straw. He also makes himself a large belly or hump with straw or hay, concealed under his blouse. He is also termed the *peilloux*, because he is clad in *peille* (rags), and finally the *pagan*, which is still more significant, because he is believed, from his cynicism and debauchery, to personify the antitheses of all the Christian virtues.

He arrives with his face smeared with soot and lees of wine, and sometimes wearing a grotesque mask. A cracked earthen cup or an old sabot, hanging to his belt by a string, serves him to ask alms of wine. No one

refuses him, and he pretends to drink, and then pours
the wine upon the earth as a libation. At every other
step he falls and rolls in the mud; he affects to be
shamefully drunk. His poor wife runs after him, picks
him up, cries for help, tears the hempen hairs which
straggle in bristling locks from her filthy head-dress,
weeps for the vileness of her husband, and reproaches
him pathetically.

"Unhappy creature!" she says, "see to what your ill
behavior has brought us! It is in vain that I spin and
labor for you, and mend your clothes; you tear and soil
them ceaselessly. You have spent my little property, our
six children are starving, we live in a stable with animals.
Here we are, reduced to asking alms; and you are so
ugly, so disgusting, so despised, that soon people will
throw bread to us as to dogs. Alas! poor people, have
pity on us; have pity on me! I have not deserved
my fate, and never had a woman a more filthy and
detestable husband. Help me to pick him up, or else
the wagons will crush him like an old potsherd, and I
shall be a widow, which will cause me to die of grief,
though every one says that it will be great good fortune
for me."

Such is the role of the gardener's wife, and her con-
tinual lamentations throughout the piece. For it is a real
comedy, free, improvised, acted in the open air, upon
the roads, over the fields, aided by all the accidental
occurrences which present themselves, and in which every
one takes part, — wedding guests and strangers, dwellers in

the houses and those who pass upon the road, — for three or four hours of the day, as will be seen. The theme is invariable, but it is elaborated to infinity; and it is in this that one may see the dramatic instinct, the abundance of droll ideas, the fertility, the spirit of repartee, and even the natural eloquence of our peasants.

The part of the gardener's wife is generally intrusted to a thin man, beardless and with a fresh complexion, who knows how to impart great truthfulness to his character, and to play burlesque despair with sufficient naturalness for people to be at once amused and saddened, as by a real event. These thin and beardless men are not rare in our country districts, and, strange to say, they are sometimes the most remarkable for muscular strength.

After the misfortunes of the wife are understood, the young men among the guests urge her to leave her husband and to divert herself with them. They offer her their arms and lead her away. By degrees she gives herself up, becomes gay, and begins to sport now with one, now with another, assuming disorderly manners, — a new *morality*, the misconduct of the husband provoking and inducing that of the wife.

Then the pagan awakes from his intoxication, looks for his companion, takes a rope and a stick and goes after her. They make him run, they hide themselves, pass the woman from one to another, and strive to distract and deceive the jealous man. His friends endeavor to intoxicate him. Finally he catches his faithless spouse and wishes to beat her. What is most real and truthful in

this parody of the miseries of conjugal life is that the
husband never attacks those who rob him of his wife.
He is very polite and prudent with them, and wishes to
find fault only with his wife, because she is supposed not
to be able to resist him.

But at the moment when he raises his stick and makes
ready his rope to bind the delinquent, all the men throw
themselves between husband and wife. " Do not beat
her! Never beat your wife!" is the formula which is
repeated to satiety in these scenes. They disarm the
husband and force him to pardon and kiss his wife, and
soon he pretends to love her better than ever. He goes
off arm-in-arm with her, singing and dancing, until a
new fit of intoxication causes him to fall; and then are
repeated the wife's lamentations, discouragement, and pretended misconduct, the husband's jealousy, the interven-
tion of the neighbors, and the reconciliation. There is in
all this a simple, even coarse lesson, which strongly savors
of its Middle-Age origin, but which always makes an
impression, if not upon the newly married couple, who
are too much in love or too reasonable in our day to
need it, at any rate upon the children and young folks.
The pagan so frightens and disgusts the young girls, by
running after them and pretending to wish to kiss them,
that they fly from him with unfeigned emotion. His dirty
face and his great stick, which is nevertheless inoffensive,
set the children to screaming. It is the comedy of manners in its most elementary but most striking stage.

When this farce is well under way, they prepare to go

in search of the cabbage. They bring a litter, upon which they place the pagan, armed with a spade, a rope, and a large basket. Four powerful men raise him upon their shoulders. His wife follows on foot, the elders follow him in a group with a grave and pensive air, and then the wedding guests follow in couples at a pace regulated by the music. The pistol-shots begin again, and the dogs bark louder than ever at the sight of the filthy pagan, thus borne in triumph.

But why this ovation for so repulsive a person? They march to the conquest of the sacred cabbage, the emblem of matrimonial fertility; and it is this brutish drunkard who alone may set his hand to the symbolic plant. No doubt there is in this a mystery earlier than Christianity, and which recalls the Saturnalia, or some ancient Bacchic festival. Perhaps this pagan, who is at the same time the ideal gardener, is nothing less than Priapus in person, the god of gardens and debauchery, — a divinity who must have been chaste and serious in his origin, like the mystery of reproduction, but whom the license of morals and the change of ideas have insensibly degraded.

However this may be, the triumphal procession reaches the bride's dwelling, and enters her garden. There they choose the finest cabbage, which is not quickly done, for the elders hold council and discuss interminably, each arguing for the cabbage which seems to him the most suitable. The matter is put to the vote, and when the choice is made, the gardener fastens his rope round the stalk, and goes off as far as the extent of the garden permits. His wife takes care that the sacred vegetable shall not be damaged in its fall. The jesters of the wedding — the hemp-dresser, the grave-digger, the carpenter, or the sabot-maker, all those, in short, who, not tilling the earth but spending their lives among others, are reputed to have, and have really, more wit and readiness than simple agricultural laborers — range themselves about the cabbage. One digs with the spade a ditch so deep that one would think they were about to cut down an oak. Another places upon his nose a pair of paper or wooden spectacles; he performs the duty of engineer, — comes, goes, makes a plan, looks at the workmen, draws lines, plays the pedant, cries that everything is being ruined, causes the work to be abandoned and resumed at his will, and directs it at as great length and as absurdly as possible. Is this an addition to the antique formula of the ceremony, in derision of theorists in general, for whom the peasant has ordinarily a sublime contempt, or from hatred of the measurers who regulate the surveys and fix the taxes, or of the civil engineers who make roads through the commons and suppress abuses dear to the peasant's heart? At any rate, this character is termed the geometer, and he does his best to make himself unendurable to those who wield the spade and pickaxe.

At last, after a quarter of an hour of objections and mummery, to avoid cutting the roots of the cabbage and to transplant it uninjured, while shovelfuls of earth are thrown in the faces of the bystanders (so much the worse for him who does not stand back quickly enough; were he bishop or prince, he would have to receive his baptism of earth), the pagan pulls the cord, his wife holds her apron, and the cabbage falls majestically amid the cheers of the spectators. Then they bring the basket, and the pagan couple plant the cabbage in it with all sorts of precautions. They surround it with moist earth, support it with sticks and strings, as town florists do to their splendid potted camellias, they stick red apples on the ends of the sticks and fasten branches of thyme, sage, and laurel about them; they bedeck the whole with ribbons and streamers, they place the trophy on the litter with the pagan, who is to keep it from falling and preserve it from accident, and finally they leave the garden in good order and at a marching pace.

But when they are about to pass the door, as well as afterwards, when they are about to enter the court of the bridegroom's house, an imaginary obstacle opposes itself. The bearers of the load stagger, utter loud exclamations, recoil, advance again, and, as if repelled by an invincible force, pretend to sink under the weight. During this time the bystanders cry, excite and calm this human team, "Get on, get on! Pull, there! Take care! Patience! Stoop, the door is too low! Close together, it is too narrow! A little to the right! Now to the left! Come, keep it up, you are almost through!"

It is thus that in years when there is a plentiful harvest the ox-cart, overladen with grain or vegetables, is too broad or too high to go through the barn door. It is thus that they cry to the vigorous animals to restrain or excite them; it is thus that with skill and violent efforts they cause the mountain of riches to pass, without being overthrown, beneath the rustic triumphal arch. It is especially the last cart, called the *gerbaude*, which requires these precautions; for it is also a rural festival, and the last sheaf taken from the last furrow is placed upon the top of the cart and ornamented with ribbons and flowers, as are the brows of the oxen and the driver's goad. Consequently, the triumphal and difficult entrance of the cabbage into the house is a symbol of the prosperity and fertility which it represents.

On arriving in the bridegroom's court-yard, the cabbage is lifted off and carried to the highest point of the house or barn. If there is a chimney, gable, or dove-cote higher than the other roofs, this burden must, at every hazard, be carried to the topmost part of the dwelling. The pagan accompanies it thither, fastens it, and waters it with a great jug of wine, while a salvo of pistol-shots and the joyful contortions of the pagan's wife signalize its inauguration.

The same ceremony is immediately repeated. They go and dig another cabbage in the bridegroom's garden, and carry it with the same formalities to the roof-tree which his wife has just left to follow him. These trophies remain until the rain and wind destroy the baskets and carry away the cabbages. But they live long enough to give some chance of success to the prediction made by the old men and matrons, as they salute it. " Fair cabbage," they say, "live and flourish, that our young bride may

bear a lovely child; for if you die too soon it will be a sign of sterility, and you will be like an evil presage up there on the roof."

The day is already well spent when all these things are accomplished. There remains only to accompany home the godfathers and godmothers of the young couple. When these putative parents live at a distance, they are attended by the musicians and all the wedding party to the boundary of the parish. There there is more dancing upon the road, and the godparents are kissed good-by. The pagan and his wife are then washed and properly dressed, when fatigue from their acting does not force them to go and take a nap.

They were still dancing, singing, and eating at the farm of Belair at midnight, this third day of the wedding, on the occasion of Germain's marriage. The old people at table could not leave, and for good reasons. They only recovered their legs and their wits the next morning at daybreak. Then, while they were returning to their homes, silent and staggering, Germain, proud and fresh, went out to hitch up his oxen, leaving his young companion to slumber until sunrise. The lark, which sang as it rose towards heaven, seemed to him the voice of his heart returning thanks to God. The hoar frost, glittering on the bare boughs, seemed to him the whiteness of April flowers preceding the appearance of the leaves. Everything in Nature was smiling and serene for him. Little Pierre had laughed and gambolled so much the day before that he did not come to help him drive his oxen; but Germain was glad to be alone. He knelt in the furrow which he was about to plough anew, and said his morning prayer with such earnestness that two tears ran down his cheeks, still moist with sweat.

In the distance could be heard the songs of the young lads of the neighboring parishes, who were setting out on their return home, and repeating in somewhat hoarse voices the joyful refrains of the day before.

AFTERWORD

i discovered a ragged copy of the andre maurois biography of george sand (LEILA) & became more curious from reading it than i had been before. i therefore tried to find books she had written herself, translated into english. the task proved impossible. the latest books of hers published in the states seems to be GRANDMOTHER TALES, published in the 30's, & now out of print. as for her novels, they were unattainable. after the educational network broadcast a series on sand, the public demand intensified, & bookstores began actively searching for her work. john wong in moe's bookstore in berkeley heard of my plans to publish her work, & saved this for me.

the early version of this book was published in 1890 by dodd, mead and company, 79 madison avenue, new york, new york, 10016. john dodd has been very kind about our project. this book is a facsimile of the original, with only minor corrections in punctuation, reproduced in its entirety. the designers at the west coast print center where this was printed suggested that i keep the original prints and color scheme; hence the red ink on the title page, and ivory inside paper and sand cover stock.

i can well imagine that in george sand's hectic life she fantasized often about a faithful, monogamous lover whose only other interest was caring for his children & plowing the earth. not to mention, love that would overcome all difficulties. this, evidently, is today an unfashionable fantasy, for the people in libraries & bookstores would often say, when excusing the fact that they had none of her works, "you aren't missing much, anyway."

this book, altho by the most famous shameless hussy we have ever published, was published in the same spirit and for the same reason as all the others; i wanted it, & there was no other way to get it. i hope the enthusiasm that drove us to this project is transmittable thru these pages, & that you find the story as enthralling as i did. if she were alive, i would speak to her about the classism (where she says workers are not as able to appreciate beauty as she is), but her social sense was accurate: she knew that workers suffered most from overwork & poverty. i thank her for sharing this picture of women of that circumstance (who were treated, it would seem, rather as household conveniences), and for a love story i can share in joyfully.

alta
shameless hussy press
april 26, 1976

/